# ROCKY ROAD & REVENGE

a Cambria Clyne mystery

Erin Huss

*To my best friend Katie Ledesma. Love you!*

## Acknowledgements:

A huge thank you to Gemma Halliday and everyone at GHP for bringing Cambria back to life. This has been a dream come true.

To my loving and supportive husband, Jed, thank you for...*well*...loving and supporting me. Natalie, Noah, Ryder, Emma, and Fisher, you are my motivation in all things. I love you.

A big thank you to my go-to defense attorney, Cody Christiansen, for the lawyer talk, and Detective *Can't-Be-Named* for the cop talk. Thank you to my beta readers—Andria Huss, Barbara Stotko, Dayna McTavish, and Julie C. Gardner. I have amazing readers who aided in the naming of characters. Thank you, Kate Murphy, Genienne Hernandez, Ashley Manis, Jessica Hughes, and Jessica Billings (rent or run dot com). To all the followers at The Apartment Manager's Blog—thank you for sticking with me all these years. My Artist's Way Group— Angie, Brooke, Holly, Kim, Michelle, and Michaela. You're all in my circle.

A massive shout-out to The Apple Store at The Oaks Mall in Thousand Oaks, California who recovered (most of) my book after my daughter spilled a glass of milk on my laptop. Sorry for hysterics. Thank you for calming me down. I've almost recovered.

Most of all, thank you to my family (Huss, Hogan, Raynaud, Stotko). I wouldn't be here without you.

Hi, Mom!
*waving*

# PROLOGUE

———

We all lie. You know it. I know it. If we're being watched by shape-shifting Lizard People, like every conspiracy theorist on Hollywood Boulevard thinks we are, then they know it too. Most are the daily lies we tell ourselves—*I can eat this cookie now because I'm starting a diet on Monday,* or *I'll shave my legs tomorrow*, or *two Diet Cokes for breakfast is totally normal.*

Other lies are disguised as secrets. Like when Tam in Apartment 7 tells his wife he's going for a run but really he's behind the maintenance garage playing Clash Royale on his phone. For me, it's the stash of Thin Mints I have hidden in my nightstand under *Pride and Prejudice*, which I've never read, never plan to. I watched the movie, once. Just so I could hold my own should I find myself in a social situation where Mr. Darcy is the topic of conversation. Which has yet to happen. Nineteenth-century literature doesn't do it for me.

For the record: eating Thin Mints does.

Some lies are earth-shattering. Like Trent's in Apartment 23. Every workday at exactly 11:15 AM a brunette in tight pants knocks on his door. Trent answers, plunges his tongue down her throat, let's her inside the apartment, and she exits an hour later looking quite pleased and mighty disheveled. Trent is married to a blonde. A blonde who thinks he's at home working all day.

Then there are the deadly lies. I'm talking if-you-knew-the-truth-I'd-have-to-kill-you type of lies. This is what makes my job interesting. As an apartment manager, I'm privy to all the secrets, all the omissions, and all the lies my residents tell. Whether I want to be or not.

It's not a job for the squeamish, hotheaded, or those with a heart condition. It's a job for me…or at least I thought it was, until I had to crawl through a burning building with a dog on my chest and bullets whizzing over my head.

Now, I'm not so sure.

I hear phlebotomy is a nice profession.

# CHAPTER ONE

———

*Property manager (n): the person charged with the care of a real estate property.*
*See also: Firefighter*

There was an urn on my desk. It wasn't one of those giant vase-looking urns, like the one my Grandma Ruthie's ashes were kept in. This one was subtle, looked more like a decoration than an urn. It was a shiny mahogany box engraved with *Mom* in swirly letters along with little flowers—forget-me-nots, if I wasn't mistaken. Ironic, since Mom had most certainly been forgotten.

I'd found the urn early that morning after a move-out inspection. Steph Woo, the now former resident of Apartment 17, was supposed to meet me at 7:00 AM for a walk-through but never showed up. Probably because her walls were painted Pepto pink and the place smelled like corn. There was little hope for a security deposit refund. She'd left the urn in her carport cabinet. I didn't know what else to do with it, so I put it on my desk and left Steph a message to come pick it up.

My name is Cambria Clyne. I'm an on-site apartment manager slash caretaker of the cremated and forgotten.

"Congratulations. You're now cursed," Amy said when I called later to tell her about my latest move-out find.

I leaned close to my computer and plugged one ear to better hear Amy over the residents passing through the lobby. "How am I cursed?"

"Harboring an urn that doesn't belong to you disturbs the deceased and causes bad luck," she said, as if this were public knowledge.

"Are you sure that's a real thing?"

"It's most certainly a real thing. You should have left it where you found it or put it in that closet by the pool. The one with all the other crap people forgot when they moved."

"If I were dead, being shoved into a storage closet would disturb me more than being placed on a desk."

"Well, you're not dead, and you have no idea how these things work." Aside from being my best friend, Amy was also an actress. She had recently landed the role of the sultry medium, Page Harrison, on the prime-time drama *Ghost Confidential* and spent much of her spare time researching the hereafter in the name of character development.

"I'm sure Steph will be back shortly to claim her mom, and all will be right in the spiritual world again," I said.

"Let's hope so. The last thing you need is bad luck."

This was true.

"Also, who forgets their mom?"

"Maybe she set it on the shelf while she loaded the car, and forgot it?" I said.

"See, that's the problems with urns. They're too portable. For the record, when I die, please have me buried at Westwood Memorial. I can't risk being misplaced."

"You don't want to be buried back home?"

"Are you kidding me? Do not bury me in Fresno. I belong in Los Angeles," she said. "There's better weather here."

"I don't think weather matters too much when you're dead. Also, Westwood is where Marilyn Monroe is buried, and Hugh Hefner, and Natalie Wood, and Farrah Fawcett and—"

"Are you on Wikipedia?"

"Maybe." *Yes.* "It sounds like a pricey place to decompose."

"That's fine. Pick a space no one wants by the fence or the freeway."

"Why are we even talking about this?" I asked. "Are you planning to die soon?"

"No, but one can never be too prepared." She exhaled into the receiver. "Anyway, I'm done shooting for the day. I'm coming by. I have to tell you about what happened to me last night, and I'll see what I can do about the urn situation."

"You realize you're not a real medium, right?"

The line went silent.

"Hello?" I glanced down at my phone's home screen: a picture of my daughter, Lilly, and me on New Year's Eve with party horns in our mouths.

Amy was gone.

I attempted a sigh. Except the dress I had on didn't offer much give for things like bending or moving or breathing or sighing. I wore it because the rusty color looked good against my pale, freckly skin, accentuated Einstein (my nickname for the dark mass of craziness springing from my head), and made my blue eyes pop.

OK, fine.

I typically wore jeans, Converse, and a T-shirt to work, but it was laundry day, and the dress was the only clean item in my closet that fit—and I use the word *fit* loosely. Or should I say *tightly*. I'd been eating my feelings as of late. I had a lot of feelings to get through. My feelings tasted like rocky road ice cream.

Whatever. I didn't have time to worry about belly rolls, spirit disturbances, or silly superstitions. I had work to do. There was a property inspection coming up, and everything had to be perfect.

Once I had a year of property management under my belt, I planned to apply for a position at a more prominent complex, one with hundreds of units, leasing agents, a full maintenance staff, and a golf cart. In my mind, if you need a golf cart to get from one end of the property to the next, you've made it.

The best way to achieve golf-cart-status was to impress the property trustee with my reports and pristine grounds and, of course, make my boss look good. These were Patrick's exact words when he called the day before to remind me that "The McMills own ninety percent of my company's portfolio. This meeting on Thursday must run smoothly. I don't want any surprises. Please make Elder Property Management look good." I got the message loud and clear and was happy to report everything was in order. The meeting would run smoothly. I would impress the trustee. All I had to do was keep it together for the next forty-eight hours, and that golf cart was as good as mine.

Next on my to-do list: the lobby.

I fluffed the couch pillows, adjusted the armchairs just so, wiped down the glass coffee table until I could see my reflection, and vacuumed the carpet. The lobby had been decorated sometime in the late eighties and not touched since. Lots of florals. Lots of stripes. Lots of neon colors. Busy wallpaper. Teal carpet. Yellow linoleum. Eucalyptus branches.

The eighties was not a good decade for home furnishings.

I'd put together a proposal to redecorate. My plan was to fuse the patterns and colors from the seventies with the deco furnishings found in many Los Angeles homes today. I thought it was an ingenious design (if I do say so myself). We *were* located in Los Angeles, and the building *was* constructed sometime in the seventies.

In my proposed revamp we'd have sleek furniture, abstract art, palms, and an orange accent wall. Patrick nearly fainted when I showed him the design. He told me it wasn't in the budget and even if it were, he'd never paint a wall orange.

So I was stuck with teal carpet and an overstuffed peach couch.

At least the lobby would smell good. I'd bought a wax warmer at Walmart and plugged it in next to the couch. It was in the shape of an owl and came with three scents. Cinnamon, linen, and apple pie.

Cinnamon was too Christmassy. Linen smelled like deodorant. Apple pie reminded me of, well, an apple pie.

Who doesn't love apple pie?

I placed three wax cubes on the tray and watched them turn to liquid. The sweet artificial scent filled the room. I grabbed my water bottle from the desk, took a seat on the ugly couch, and crossed my legs. It was quiet. Lilly had gone with her dad, Tom, for the day, and it was near closing time, which meant most residents would use the pedestrian gate instead of walking through the lobby.

I threw my hands behind my head, sat back, and had a look around. Sure the lobby was offensive to the eyes, but it was home, and the perfect setup for a single mom like myself. To the right was my enclosed office with a waist-high counter (also teal, also ugly) overlooking the lobby, where I could work and chat with the residents who walked through. The door behind my desk opened to my attached two-bedroom apartment. I could be working one minute, turn around, step into the kitchen, and make— *That doesn't smell right?*

\* \* \*

Random fact: if a wax warmer catches on fire, dousing it with water causes a *bigger* fire. Also, 1980s furniture is quite flammable.

The emergency service personnel hustled to and from the wreckage while I watched the scene unfold from the street. "Mom" was safe in my hands. I'd wrapped the urn in a sweatshirt for protection before I rushed out of the building. If moving an urn disturbed the deceased, then lighting one on fire could have eternal consequences. Not that I really believed in all that.

It didn't take long for a group of residents to congregate on the driveway. Their breaths huffed out in white clouds against the darkening sky as they chattered about their manager, who had just burned down the building. Which technically wasn't true. The building was still erect. The lobby was just a bit crispy now. However, Silvia Kravitz stood in the middle of the crowd with her parrot, Harold, perched on her shoulder, and by this time tomorrow I'd be a pyromaniac who burned down the building.

Silvia was the Mayor of Rumorville, with Harold as her deputy. She'd started a rumor last year that I had a threesome with the retired couple in Apartment 22. You could read all about it on Yelp, Apartment Ratings, Rent or Run dot com, and *Superior Senior Living*.

So now I was a pyromaniac with a geriatric fetish.
*Meh.*

I'd been called worse.

I approached the group of residents on shaky legs. My nerves were fried. Silvia folded her arms and tapped her foot. Silvia Kravitz was a retired actress who looked like the seventy-year-old love child of Gollum and Joan Rivers. And she only wore lingerie: no matter the time of day, the occasion, or whether or not the sun was at the perfect angle to blast through the sheer fabric.

"A faulty wax warmer caught fire, and the damage was contained to the lobby," I said to them. "No apartments were involved."

"What about smoke inhalation?" Silvia said with a theatrical wave of her hand.

Harold turned his backside to me. Everyone standing around her nodded and whispered "good point" to each other.

"Excuse me?"

Silvia draped an arm around Shanna, the new resident in Apartment 15. "This poor young dear has an audition tomorrow, and how is she to sing with smoke-filled lungs?"

Shanna let out a dainty cough.

Heaven help me. I had too many actors in my life.

I assured everyone the best way to avoid smoke inhalation was to go home and close the doors. Two out of fifteen residents listened to their property manager. Which was about the national average.

As the firefighters left and the trucks disappeared, the crowd eventually thinned. Residents lost interest and went back to their apartments. Which was good, because I still had to call Patrick.

He freaked.

"Look at the couch!" I had him on FaceTime so he could see the damage for himself. The fire inspector had deemed the structure sound and allowed me back in. The office was smoky but not charred. My apartment was smelly but fine. Other than that, it wasn't so bad.

OK, fine. That's a lie.

It was terrible. I had the trustee inspection in two days, and I'd just burned down the lobby! The back wall was singed, the couch unrecognizable, the beams were exposed, ash rained down, the once teal carpet was black, and firefighters had busted one window.

At least no one was hurt, and the lobby would get a new look after all?

I had to find the silver lining to keep from crying.

"It's a nightmare!" Patrick wasn't a silver-lining kind of guy. "You'll need to board the window and call the insurance, and we'll need a restoration company out there tonight."

"Done. Done, and done," I said. "The restoration company will be here in an hour. I left a message with the claims department, and Mr. Nguyen is out buying wood for the window." Mr. Nguyen was the maintenance man. We couldn't pronounce his first name, so we kept it formal. "You don't have to worry. I'll take care of everything." I gave what I hoped was a reassuring smile.

Patrick responded with a grunt. We hung up with a promise that I wouldn't burn anything else down.

I sighed the best I could in my restrictive clothing. What a mess. I picked up a seared throw pillow with my forefinger and thumb. My eyes cut over to "Mom." She was back on the desk, sitting between the stapler and the ancient answering machine. I thought about what Amy had said...

Before I could dwell too much on the paranormal, Chase showed up. Chase Cruller (as in the donut) was once the maintenance man. He was now a detective for the great city of Los Angeles. Which kept him busy. There were a lot of criminals around these parts.

Chase was also *sort of* my boyfriend. He has dark blond hair, green eyes, a five o'clock shadow no matter the time of day, rock-solid abs, and I'm pretty sure he could be an underwear model if he weren't busy fighting bad guys.

He sidestepped the debris to avoid dirtying his shiny shoes. He had on a gray tailored suit and black tie, the outfit reserved for super-official detective duty.

"What are you doing here?" I asked him.

"I saw the fire trucks driving down Sepulveda and had a strange hunch they were coming from your place." He looked around, taking in the new landscape of the lobby. "What happened?"

"The wax warmer caught on fire, so I doused it with my water, and it caught on fire more."

"That's unfortunate." He brushed a fallen ash off his sleeve.

"Very. So why are you so formal?" I tugged on the lapels of his jacket "Funeral or press conference?"

"Press conference?" Chase narrowed his eyes. "You haven't heard the news?"

"Been a little busy." I waved to the crispy lobby. "Why? What happened?"

"Jessica Wilders was murdered."

I gasped.

"Her assistant found her at home this morning with multiple gunshot wounds."

I gasped.

"Wasn't pretty."

Jessica Wilders was the star of *Ghost Confidential*. Amy would argue there was no "star," that it was an ensemble, but that was only because she couldn't stand Jessica—who was the star. Jessica was a skeletal brunette with dark eyes and a gap between her two front teeth—what she was known for. She played Lola Darling, a ghost trapped in the body of her ex-husband's new wife, who was also her killer's sister. It was gripping television.

I'd met Jessica at a cast party once. I'd tagged along as Amy's last-minute date. Her boyfriend had to work late because "he's a *doc-tor*," Amy had announced upon arrival. About thirty minutes into the night, I'd managed a short but meaningful conversation with Jessica. She asked me where the bathroom was because she thought I worked there. Too starstruck to form words, I pointed a crab leg toward the commodes. This was the extent of our interaction, and now she was dead.

"That's horrible. Do you have any idea who killed her?" asked Chase.

"No suspects and no solid leads right now, but we'll get there," he said.

I wondered how Amy had taken the news. Come to think of it…*where is Amy?* She said she was coming over, and that was hours ago.

Chase checked his watch. "I have to head to the station now. This is the highest-profile case I've ever worked so…"

"I'll see you when I see you." I hid my disappointment with a smile. "No worries. Go catch the killer, and I'll be here, trying not to burn anything else down."

Chase pulled me closer and tucked a strand of Einstein behind my ear. "Thank you for understanding."

"Of course." I wrapped my arms around his waist. I could feel the holster on his hip. I'm not going to lie—knowing he was packing heat was kind of hot. "You can make it up to me later."

"Oh yeah?" A devilish grin spread across his face. "What did you have in mind?"

"Gee, I don't know. Let me think about it." I played coy. The man knew what I wanted.

Chase leaned in and kissed me. His stubble was rough against my face, but his lips were sweet and firm. My legs went to goo.

"Is this what you had in mind?" he whispered against my mouth.

"Actually, I was going to say ice cream, pizza, and the latest Liam Neeson movie, but this is a good start."

Chase laughed. "I'll call you tomorrow."

"You better." I gave him a playful smack on the rear.

Chase sidestepped the debris on his way to the door, when in came Tom, with Lilly at his side.

Oh geez.

Tom Dryer (as in the appliance) was my one-night-stand turned baby daddy. He was a criminal defense attorney. Does mostly pro bono work. Which kept him busy. There were a lot of poor criminals around these parts.

If you squinted and tilted your head to the side, Tom looked like a tall Dylan McDermott. He could probably be an underwear model too. My parents thought he was gay. But the hundred or so women he'd slept with over the course of his lifetime would attest otherwise.

Tom was wearing basketball shorts, a Lakers tee, sandals, and a frown.

He wasn't my *sort of* boyfriend. Tom didn't do relationships. There were feelings there. He knew it. I knew it. Chase knew it. No one talked about it. Which made this reunion *sort of* awkward.

Blissfully unaware of the tension in the air, Lilly ran up and wrapped her arms around my legs. I swung her on my hip and gave her a kiss on the cheek. "What happens to the lobby?" she asked.

"What *happened* was there was a fire." I swept a dark curl off her forehead. "There were *three* fire trucks here."

Lilly's hazel eyes went wide. "Did you get to ride in one?"

"Not this time."

"Wow, Cam." Tom stepped in further and stood beside Chase. They acknowledged each other with a quick jerk of their chins. "You OK?"

"I'm fine. It was a silly mishap." I giggled what was supposed to be an endearing giggle but sounded more like an old-lady cackle. 'Cause I'm smooth like that.

"Oh no!" Lilly slapped her forehead. "Are my dolls OK?"

"I think they are. Why don't you go check."

Lilly scrambled to break free from my grasp and ran into the apartment. The situation became fifty times more uncomfortable without the toddler buffer around.

"So…" I rocked from heel to toe. "How 'bout them Dodgers?"

Chase shoved his hands into the front pockets of his slacks. "They choked in the World Series."

"I hardly call losing in game seven a choke job."

I'd forgotten how much Tom loved his Dodgers. And how much Chase didn't love the Dodgers. He was an Angels fan.

Bad icebreaker.

"Um…so, Jessica Wilders is dead." 'Cause murder is a better icebreaker?

Honestly.

*Note to self: you suck at icebreakers.*

"I heard about that." Tom turned to Chase. "Are you working the case?"

Chase nodded his head.

"That should take up a lot of your time." Tom perked up and looked at me. "I'll call you tomorrow."

Oh geez. I had no idea how to handle so much male attention.

I pulled at my collar. "You know what? I have to clean up this mess and call Amy to be sure she's OK."

I ushered the two outside. "Thank you for stopping by. Take care. Talk to you later." I closed the door and locked it, which did little good since the window was missing and I could hear the two arguing baseball outside.

I grabbed my phone and called Amy. It went straight to voicemail. Even if Amy and Jessica Wilders didn't get along, I knew Amy would be devastated. I tried calling her again. It went straight to voicemail.

I sent a text.

*Heard about Jessica. Are you OK?*

# CHAPTER TWO

------

*See also: Exterminator*

The next morning I awoke with a gasp, imagining Jessica Wilders had snuck into my apartment and beat me on the back of the head with the urn while Chase and Tom stood by in their underwear and watched.

It was the sexiest nightmare I'd ever had.

I should have skipped the midnight ice cream binge.

The clock claimed it was 7:00 AM. The time confirmed when the ceiling creaked. It was my upstairs neighbor Mickey performing his morning bathroom march. Then came the *swoosh* of the toilet, slam of the seat, *psshhhh* of the sink, and *thud* of him hurling himself back into bed, just as he did every freaking morning.

There was no point going back to sleep. Lilly would be awake soon, and it was March 1. I pulled the covers up to my chin, threw my hands behind my head, and waited.

My phone buzzed from the nightstand. I didn't have to look to know it was my mom calling. Every year on March 1, at exactly 7:01 AM, my mother called to tell me the story of a teenager from Fresno who endured a long, drug-free labor only to have an emergency C-section because her baby had an "unusually large head."

That's right. March 1 is my birthday.

Which meant two things:

One: I'd spent nearly three decades on this planet and still had no clue what I was doing.

Two: my birthday would always and forever land on rent day.

I let the call go to voicemail. Not because I didn't want to talk to my mom, and not because I didn't enjoy hearing about my gigantic noggin and my mother's dainty lady bits (as lovely a visual as that was). Jessica Wilders had just murdered me in my sleep. Amy had yet to call me back. The lobby had burned down. I had the inspection tomorrow. I was a *wee* bit stressed. If I answered, she'd hear the angst in my voice and ask what was wrong. Not just ask either. She'd hound me until I broke, and I hadn't exactly been forthcoming about my troubles since moving to Los Angeles.

My parents had divorced when I was eight years old, and even though my dad remarried, neither went on to have more kids. So it wasn't as if I had siblings to take some of the pressure off. Like—*Cambria is a hot mess, but luckily we have another child to rest our unfulfilled life wishes on.*

It was part of the reason my parents thought Tom was gay. When I told them I was pregnant, the conversation went like this:

Mom (rolling eyes): "This isn't some guy you picked up at a bar, is it?"

Dad: "Oh no, Cambria."

Me: "No! We were together...kind of." For about fifteen minutes. After we left the bar.

Dad: "Were?"

Mom: "Great. Another man who can't stick it out for the sake of his kid." She shot my dad an evil eye. I couldn't have her giving Tom the same eye. It would make my baby's life miserable.

Me: "It's not like that. I'm just...not his type." As in, I wasn't a slut—though previous actions would suggest otherwise.

Mom: "Ohhhhh, I get it. I saw something like this on *Dr. Phil.*"

Dad and Me: "Huh?"

Mom: "Kids who are raised by a straight mother and a gay father. It makes for a well-balanced child."

Should I have corrected her? Probably. But if I had, my mom would have thought Tom was a horrible parent for not attempting to keep his family together, when in reality he was a doting father. Lilly was lucky to have him. So I kept my mouth shut, and now my mom loved Tom. She marched in the Gay Pride Parade every year in his honor.

Sometimes it's vital to withhold information for the well-being of your baby daddy.

My phone buzzed again. I knew it wasn't Amy. She didn't wake up this early. It was Dad. I could deal with Dad. He didn't study the fluctuation of my voice the way my mom did.

He was already on the second chorus of *Happy Birthday* when I answered. My dad had a jolly voice. It didn't matter if you were his child or the mailman—he spoke to everyone like they were the most important person in the world.

"Thanks, Dad," I said.

"I didn't wake you, did I?"

I sat up slowly and readjusted my pillow for better back support. "No, I was awake. How are you doing?"

"We're good. Work's been slow, but my boys have been on a winning streak." My dad coached the varsity boys' basketball team at the high school. "Rebecca took over the debate team, and that's kept her busy."

Rebecca is the woman my dad married. She was my high school Spanish teacher—a five-foot-nothing blonde who sounded as if she were on a helium drip. It didn't matter if you were her stepdaughter or the janitor—she spoke to everyone like they were the janitor.

"Tell me what's going on with you, kiddo. How's work?"

"It's *going*. There's an inspection tomorrow—"

"Is that Cambria on the phone?" Rebecca shrieked in the background.

*Oh no.*

"Can I talk to her?" she asked.

*Say no. Say no. Say no.*

Not that I didn't want to speak to Rebecca.

OK fine. I didn't want to speak to Rebecca.

She'd managed to commandeer any and all father-daughter time since she *entrado en mi vida*.

"Calvin! Let me have the phone!"

Yes, my dad's name was Calvin, and yes my last name was Clyne. And of course his plumbing business was called Calvin Clyne Plumbing, with a picture of my dad recreating a classic black and white Calvin Kline ad with his jeans on, smolder in place, and a plunger slung over his shoulder. It made high school real fun.

"*Feliz cumpleaños*, Cambria!"

*Ouch, my eardrum.*

"I can't believe how big you've gotten!"

"Gee, thanks, Rebecca."

"I've been watching the news. I can't believe Jessica Wilders was murdered. Does Amy know anything?"

I sunk back down and pulled the comforter over my head. "I don't think so. Can I talk to my dad?"

"'Cause you know, I tell all my students that I used to teach Amy Magnolia. One of the stars of *Ghost Confidential*!"

Guest star, but whatever.

"I'm curious if the show can go on without Lola Darling."

"I don't know. Is my dad there?"

"What will happen between Lola and Frank? Can you ask Amy for me?"

"Sure. Lola and Frank…*hello?*…*hello?*…poor connection…*I…ju…got*

…*to…so…nice…talk*—" *Click.*

It was my birthday, and if I wanted to hang up on the woman my dad married, then I could. Except, *crap*, I felt guilty about it.

Not guilty enough to call her back.

I sent Amy another two texts then rolled out of bed and shuffled to go pee and weigh myself. The morning rays peeked through the blinds, and tiny dust particles danced in the light. Lilly called them "morning sparkles."

Even though I'd lived there five months, there were still unlabeled moving boxes stacked in the corner. Next to my bed was a red antique nightstand that a tenant had left behind when he'd moved. Above my bed was a framed picture of the Los Angeles landscape, also left behind by a move-out. California required me to store the discarded belongings for thirty days before I could get rid of them (aka use them as décor in my apartment).

There was a cherrywood television stand in the storage closet that had fifteen days left. I'd already claimed it.

Pushed up against the wall by the patio door was the giant wooden armoire the previous manager Joyce had left behind when she moved. It was empty, smelled like nicotine, and had to be dismantled before it could be hauled away. So, it stayed.

In short, my style was made up of other people's trash. Except for my bed. My bed was new. I'd used my Christmas bonus to buy a mattress and frame. It was big and modern and sleek and didn't match anything else in my apartment. But it felt like I was sleeping on a cloud of marshmallows. Or so I assumed.

In the bathroom, I stood at the sink and examined my face in the mirror. I didn't look any older. Tired? Sure. Pale? Always. Older? Not really.

*What the…* I leaned in closer. Why is adult acne even a thing? Like teenage acne wasn't bad enough, here were a dozen painful whiteheads to carry you through your twenties.

*It's not right.*

I put a headband on and slathered my face with soap. I thought about Jessica Wilders. Multiple gunshot wounds? What an awful way to die. Who would do that? How would they do it? I wouldn't consider Jessica an A-list celebrity, but she was at least a B+. She was well known but didn't grace the cover of tabloids like Jennifer Aniston or Brad Pitt did. Still, I was sure she lived in a gated community with cameras. It was weird that Amy hadn't said anything to me about it. Not a text. Not a phone call. Nothing.

I thought back to our last conversation. Amy said that she had something to tell me. I had serious doubt *that* something was the murder of her co-worker. She was too casual about it and—

A bloodcurdling scream came from Lilly's room. "Help! Emergency!"

Frantic, I scrambled to find a towel, blindly feeling around the counter. My hand landed on something cloth-like, and I bolted, wiping the soap from my eyes.

"Momma, hurry!" Lilly cried.

I stumbled through her door, tripped on a toy car, and went butt first into Lilly's Barbie castle—taking out the roof and landing on a Ken.

"What happened?" I struggled to my feet and took note of the fact that I was wiping my face with the shirt I'd planned to wear that day.

"There's a spider!" She pointed to a black piece of fluff on the ground.

"Oh, sweetie." I half laughed, half sighed in relief, half cried because of the soap burning my cornea, and bent down to pick up the offending piece of fluff. "It's only— *Ahhhh!* It's a spider!" Not just any spider either. It was a giant tarantula with fur, native to Mars.

I screamed. Lilly screamed. I screamed. Lilly screamed louder. The spider raised its front legs, ready to attack. I used a book to scoop it up and dumped the mutant on the patio, along with the book, and locked the door.

It was traumatic.

Good thing I had donuts to take our minds off it. A birthday treat I'd bought for myself the night before. Donuts for breakfast was a Clyne family tradition that I started, that day.

Forgetting all about the spider, Lilly went for a sprinkled glaze while I opted for a swig of Mylanta. My throat burned, and I felt like hairy legs were crawling up my back and down my arms…

*Blah-aha-aha-aha.*

"Am I seeing Daddy today?" Lilly asked from the table. Her little legs swung beneath her while she ate.

"I'm not sure." I turned around to check the time on the stove. 7:30 AM.

"What am I doing today then?" she asked.

"You get to hang out with Mrs. Nguyen this morning while I do some work."

"So you can get ready for the owner ingest-tion?"

"*Inspection.* Well, really it's the trustee, not the owner." I poured Lilly a glass of almond milk and placed it next to her plate.

She took a sip and licked her milk mustache away. "Momma, what's a trust-eee?"

"That's a good question." I had to think about how to explain this to a three-year-old. "So when you're really old and really rich and don't feel like dealing with your millions of dollars and big property investments anymore, you hire someone to handle it all for you. That's a trustee. He makes sure the really old and really rich people stay really rich."

"Momma, why do you call a fairy that doesn't shower?"

"Oh." *Guess we're moving on.* "I don't know. *What* do you call a fairy that doesn't shower?"

"A stinkerbell!" She giggled, and milk spewed out of her nose.

I handed her a napkin. "That's a good one. Hey, why did the chicken cross the playground?"

"Why? Why? Why?" Her eyes went wide in joyful anticipation.

*I love her.*

"To get to the other slide!" I laughed at my wittiness.

Lilly did not.

"Oh come on. Get to the other *slide* instead of the other side? That's funny."

She shook her head. "No, it's not."

I'm not going to lie—that stung. "Normally, it's the chicken crosses the road to get to the other *side*, but in this joke it's *slide* because it's a playground, and playgrounds have slides. It's a play on words." If you had to explain the punch line, the joke was a dud. But I continued anyway. "The chicken didn't cross the road. He crossed the playground."

My lame joke was interrupted by a knock on the door. Lilly and I looked at each other and smiled. It was Tom. Or Chase. Hopefully not both. Unless they were in their underwear. Then I might not mind so much.

Or it was a resident who'd locked himself out.

Probably a resident.

Hopefully, *he* wasn't in his underwear.

I turned off the alarm, unlocked the deadbolt, swung open the door, and… "Kevin?"

# CHAPTER THREE

---

*See also: Budtender*

Kevin pushed past me, dropped his bag on the couch, and kicked off his shoes as if he were home. His auburn hair was slicked back and peppered with more gray hairs than I remembered. The studs in his ears were gone. His complexion was brighter, and his demeanor steady. He looked good. And it was hard to look good in a gray sweat suit.

"Tom, by the way, is an awesome attorney," he said. "Got me out of rehab. Just had to do my time, and now I'm clean as a whistle." He whistled to add to the effect.

"What a surprise to see you..." I closed the door slowly, weighted by shock. He wasn't supposed to be home for another two months. "Welcome back."

"It's good to be back." Kevin brought his hands to his hips and looked around. It was the first time he'd been inside my apartment. Prior to his drug conviction, we weren't on the friendliest of terms. During most of our encounters, he was high, and loud, and belligerent, and naked. I wasn't a big Kevin fan. Once I'd learned his backstory, my opinion of him softened. Over twenty years ago, his parents (the really old and really rich owners of the building) exiled him here after they found out he was gay. The deal was he didn't have to pay rent, or utilities, and could do whatever he wanted so long as he didn't contact them. My single thread of hope for their sense of humanity was that they'd sent Kevin to their favorite property.

Kevin and I had exchanged letters while he was locked up, and I now considered us on friendly terms—friendly enough for me to finally introduce him to my daughter.

"Lilly, this is Kevin. He lives in Apartment 40," I said.

Lilly waved a donut.

"Hey, kid." Kevin took a seat at the table and grabbed a maple-glazed bar. "Don't be an idiot when you grow up."

Lilly shrugged her little shoulders. "OK."

"And never go to prison. It sucks."

"What's prison?"

"It's where you can get any STD you want."

Her little mouth fell open. "Ohhh, I want an STD."

"No you don't!" I clapped my hands. "So, um, Kevin, have you been to your apartment yet?"

"No." He licked maple off his fingertips. "I came here first because you have the key."

*Oh, right.*

"Let me get it for you." I went to the office and grabbed his key from the safe. *Mom* was right where I left her. I thought about my dream and rubbed the back of my head.

"Is that an *urn*?" Kevin asked from the office doorway. He was now working on an old-fashioned glazed.

"Yes. A resident left it behind when they moved."

"Saw something about urns on that show *Ghost Confidential*. Harboring one that doesn't belong to you disturbs the deceased and causes bad luck."

"I don't think that's a real thing."

"Maybe. But Lola Darling messed with an urn in last week's episode then got knocked off in real life yesterday. My Uber driver told me all the details. Sounds gruesome."

"Yeah, I heard it wasn't pretty." I checked my phone. Almost 8:00 AM and still no word from Amy.

Lilly skipped in, crawled into my chair, and began spinning. Her favorite activity.

"So what's with the lobby?" Kevin pointed with his chin. "You redecorating?"

I followed his gaze. The window was boarded up with wood. The furniture was gone. The restoration company had removed the drywall and carpet. They'd also set up air scrubbers and hydroxyl machines that made the air smell less like smoke and more like chemicals.

"A wax melt caught on fire and took the lobby with it." I dropped the keys to Kevin's apartment into his hand. "Welcome home."

Kevin arched an eyebrow. "I assume you have everything in order?"

I nodded. He had asked me in a letter to fix his window, which was a huge step. Last year he'd broken it while in the midst of a drug-induced tantrum. If only he'd let me fix the rest of his apartment. It was a tweaker haven in there—nonsensical writings on the wall, ripped-up flooring, and missing cabinets. Barbies pinned to the wall with knives. The front door was black with the *forty* sprayed in red, dripping paint. And don't get me started on the mildew smell, but I no longer trusted air fresheners.

"The window is fixed, and I didn't touch anything else," I assured him.

"And you fed Viper?"

"Sure did." Viper was his snake. He ate one mouse a week. Talk about traumatizing.

"Got my mail?"

"It's on the headless statue by the door."

"Took care of my plants?"

"Errmm…" I tugged at the bottom of my shirt. "They…*died*."

"What!"

"Kevin, when you asked me to take care of your plants, I assumed you meant a houseplant. But you had—" I glanced at Lilly, who was on her third go-around in the chair. "You had a m-a-r-i…j?" *Never mind.* "You had w-e-e-d plants. Do you know how hard it is to take care of those?" I might have googled it. "And do you really think it's a good idea to have pot around when you're on p-a-r-o-l-e?"

"First." He held up one finger. "Stop spelling at me. Second." He held up two fingers. "Pot is legal now. And fourth." He held up four fingers. "Wait…what number was I—"

"Third."

"That's right. *Third*, I had a nice side business going on. What am I supposed to do for money now?" he asked in a way that insinuated this was now my problem.

"Get a job?"

He looked appalled, as if I'd just proposed he grow fins and become a show whale.

"Momma has a job," Lilly chimed in, still spinning. "She has owner incest tomorrow."

"Inspection! She means inspection," I quickly mended.

Kevin's face skewed into a question mark. "My parents are coming? Why would they come? They haven't been here in decades."

"No, no, no, noooooo. It's the trustee. He's coming," I winced, afraid of how this news would jolt his newly sober heart.

Kevin's lips went to a line. I thought he was about to cry, until he folded in half and wheezed with laughter.

*He's cracked.*

"The...trustee...Trevor..." Kevin said between gasps of laughter. "He's going to...eat...you...alive."

*Wait, what?*

"I have color-coded reports," I said, feeling defensive, and pointed to the manila folders on my desk to prove it.

Kevin rolled upright and rubbed at his eyes. "Wow, I haven't laughed this hard in a long time."

"I'm glad me getting eaten alive is so funny." I crossed my arms. "Why is he going to eat me alive?"

"Trevor is..." Kevin leaned against the desk while he searched for the right adjective. "*Interesting*," he decided. "He's my cousin. On my dad's side. Total nut. He graduated from some nut law school and talked my parents into letting him run their wealth. I don't trust him. He's a nut."

"Your cousin?" First I heard of this news. "And a nut? How so?"

Kevin picked at his back teeth. "He's...a...a nut. There's no other word for it. Says I have negative energy." He shrugged. "Could be true. Not sure what he'll think of you. You talk a lot. I'd work on that."

"No I don't." OK, maybe a little, but only when I was nervous. Like during interviews, public speaking, doctor's appointments, and meetings with authoritative figures.

I choked on my own spit.

How had I not factored this into my preparations for tomorrow?

If *Merriam-Webster* were to define *me*, it'd say:

*Cambria (came-bree-ah) Jane Clyne.*

*1. Awkward, overshares, nosey, says the word* crap *a lot, talks too much when nervous, not a good first-impression-maker, klutz, and overthinker.*

Crap. Crap. Crap.

# CHAPTER FOUR

———

*See also: Surveillance*

OK, so maybe it would be harder to impress the trustee, make Patrick look good, and get my golf cart than I originally thought. Which was fine because I had devised a plan.

Plan: clean the upstairs railings.

I didn't say it was good one.

But it was either take action or stress-eat ice cream. And I was trying this new thing where I didn't gain a pound a day. My clothes were about to stage an intervention.

Would cleaner railings make a difference? Like Trustee Trevor would say, "Wow, the apartment manager is obnoxious and starts fires, but the railings are superb. She's a keeper!"

Probably not, but it was the next thing on my to-do list, and Mr. Nguyen was busy installing the new lobby window.

First, Lilly and I stopped by Amy's apartment to check on her.

Amy lived in the third courtyard in Apartment 36 with her boyfriend, Spencer. The two had been cohabitating since the New Year. The second rule in property management is: be friendly with everyone and make friends with no one. (The first rule is: don't rent to drug dealers. I learned that lesson the hard way.) But Spencer was a resident before he was my best friend's boyfriend, and Amy had been my best friend since the third grade. I'd told myself that the rule was null and void for this situation and hoped it wouldn't come back to bite me in the rear.

I knocked on the door.

Lilly knocked.

I knocked.

Lilly pounded her little fists.

No answer.

I knew Amy was home. Her car was in the carport. I peeked in through the window. The television was on, muted, and turned to *Good Morning America*. A picture of Jessica Wilders' face filled the screen, with *Inside Job?* printed on the bottom. The microwave was lit up with two minutes left, and a tub of sugar-free, carb-free, gluten-free, dairy-free, taste-free ice cream was open on the counter—Amy's stress food of choice.

I understood her not talking to the press, but Amy and I talked about everything. She'd call me in a panic if there was a zit on her nose. So why not call when her costar turned up dead? It didn't make sense.

In my worst-case-scenario mind: the person who killed Jessica came for Amy, and she was inside her apartment—dead.

But I was trying this new thing where I didn't allow the worst-case-scenario part of my brain to take over.

In my logical mind: Amy couldn't be dead, because then who was using the microwave? Not Spencer. He'd left for work early that morning. The reason I'd yet to hear from Amy was because she'd been advised by her agent to keep a low profile and not speak to *anyone.* Her phone was off, and she was probably running a bath. Amy obsessively groomed when she was stressed.

I wedged a note into her doorframe, asking her to call me when she could talk about it.

\* \* \*

Mr. and Mrs. Nguyen (pronounced "when") lived in an upstairs apartment in the third courtyard, next door to "Grandma" Clare and Bob in Apartment 22. The two elderly residents Silvia had accused me of trio-ing with last year. They sounded as if they were enjoying their afternoon. Despite my requests, they still hadn't moved their headboard from against the wall.

I knocked on Mrs. Nguyen's door and placed my hands over Lilly's ears while Grandma Clare and Bob…*errr…ahhh…*finished.

Mrs. Nguyen answered. She wiped her hands on the apron tied around her tiny waist. She was making pho. I could smell the beefy broth and spices simmering.

"Come inside. We start making lunch."

"*Tôi đói,*" Lilly replied and skipped across the threshold.

Mrs. Nguyen looked me over and frowned. "You look bad!"

She wasn't a beat-around-the-bush kind of woman. I appreciated this about her, usually.

I glanced down at my flannel shirt and jeans. "They're my cleaning clothes."

"No. It your face. It's too pale!" Both Mr. and Mrs. Nguyen were hard of hearing. Which made them the perfect neighbors for Grandma Clare and Bob, who were…*errr…ahhh*…loud. "You need to eat more meat!"

This was Mrs. Nguyen's answer to everything.

"I will," I said. "And thanks again for watching Lilly this morning. I really appreciate it."

Mrs. Nguyen brushed off my gratitude. She loved Lilly like she was her own. She and Mr. Nguyen had been my next-door neighbors way back when, before I was an apartment manager. They'd known Lilly since the day I brought her home from the hospital. We called them Lilly's SoCal grandparents since my parents lived four hours away in Fresno and Tom's lived in Tahoe. Again, not supposed to rent to friends, but Mr. Nguyen was the maintenance man. Living here was part of the job.

"You hear about that actress who died?" Mrs. Nguyen leaned against the doorjamb and crossed her arms. "Wasn't she on that show with Amy?"

I nodded. "Jessica Wilders. She played Lola Darling."

"Such a shame. She was too skinny but too young to die. How Amy doing?"

"Not sure." I glanced over my shoulder down to Amy's apartment. The blinds were now drawn, and my note was still stuck in the door. "Truth is, I haven't spoken to her yet."

Mrs. Nguyen's eyes widened. "You not talked to her? OK, I don't feel so bad then. I try to bring her food last night, but she didn't answer."

"What time?"

"It was after you burned down the lobby. Around seven thirty, and then again at eight, and eight fifteen. I stopped trying around ten."

"For the record, I didn't *burn* down the lobby. And are you sure she was home?"

"I'm sure. I see her come home. She was on the phone and ran across the grass and slammed the door."

*Huh.*

"She's probably not allowed to talk to anyone about it right now." At least that was my best guess. "I'll let her know you have food when I talk to her."

"Good. And…wait. Hold on. I have something for you," Mrs. Nguyen said, suddenly remembering. "Stay there. I'll be back."

*Oh, right, birthday.*

Lilly was already at the table with a coloring book and a box of crayons. I leaned against the doorframe and waited. I hoped Mrs. Nguyen wasn't about to give me a gift because one: I didn't want her spending money on me. Two: my brain shut down at the sight of wrapping paper. I get embarrassed and squeaky. Amy, on the other hand, was a gracious gift receiver. Her eyes lit up, her face got big, and she made you feel as if you were the most amazing person in the world who had bestowed upon her the very thing she'd ever wanted. Then returned it the following day. Must be all the acting classes she'd taken when we first moved to LA.

*Note to self: google awkward-people classes.*

Mrs. Nguyen returned with Lilly's pink sequined sweater and no present. "I fixed the hole in arm. It's good now."

She handed it to me. I ran my finger over the nearly invisible stitching. Lilly had ripped it on a bush in the breezeway. She'd cried and mumbled—what I'd hoped wasn't profanity—in Vietnamese. Santa Claus had brought it for her, and it was her "*most favorite thing ever.*"

"My sweater is fixed!" Lilly cheered from her spot at the table. She had a serious love of clothes, shoes, and all accessories. Not a trait she'd inherited from me. "I can't believe you fixed it."

Lilly ran from the kitchen and wrapped her arms around Mrs. Nguyen's waist. Mrs. Nguyen pushed a curl behind Lilly's ear, and the two conversed in Vietnamese. I rocked from heel to toe and waited for a break in the conversation to say, "OK, I'll leave you two alone." I thanked Mrs. Nguyen again and gave her a hug. Her head barely cleared my chest.

"You welcome. Now go, go, and get to work. Get ready for tomorrow's big meeting." She took Lilly's hand and closed the door without another word.

Not one...or two.

It was OK. I didn't need a "happy birthday" from Mrs. Nguyen or—I checked my phone—*anyone.*

Whatever. I had railings to clean.

I strolled through the third courtyard. It was a beautiful day—seventy-five degrees and not a cloud in the sky. The brownish-greenish grass glistened with morning dew. The pool sparkled blue. The birds chirped. After a semi-cold winter, the Boston ivy lacing the breezeways was no longer sparsely leafed twisted branches, but rather green-leafed twisted branches. In a month or two, the breezeways would bloom into a lush hallway covered in leaves and tiny flowers. It was the only greenery on the property, due to Los Angeles's stringent water restrictions.

California was in a perpetual drought.

I passed my upstairs neighbor Mickey, who was stuttering to himself—something about government conspiracies and corrupt cops—the usual. He spent most of the day wandering around the property. Per his file, he was a retired mailman, but in my romanticized mind, he was an ex-member of the CIA and the mailman was nothing but a cover. He was a nice guy. A little odd. OK, a lot odd. He'd lived there over twenty years. We'd had a few conversations. He hadn't offered too much personal information, mostly asked me about myself. Total ex-CIA move.

In the breezeway, Silvia stopped me to complain about her neighbor Larry. Then Larry stopped me to complain about his latest colonoscopy and persistent gas pains. Apartment 5's garbage disposal "is making a *gggggggg* noise when I flip it on." Apartment 20's doorknob "won't turn to the left."

I sent Mr. Nguyen the work orders, explained to Silvia that I could not ask Larry not to flush his toilet before 6:00 AM, and reminded Larry that I was not qualified to give medical advice. I walked out to the maintenance garage and found Tam from Apartment 7 in his usual spot, hiding from his wife and playing on his phone. Tam was a pudgy guy who was on a rigorous weight-loss plan ordered by his doctor and enforced by his wife. The plan called for a brisk jog four days a week. And four days a week, I found him hiding behind the maintenance garage, decked in shorts and a tank top, with a sweatband around his head, playing video games on his phone.

"Good morning, Tam."

"Hi, Cambria," Tam replied without looking up.

"How many miles are you supposed to be jogging today?"

"I'm up to three and a half." He stuck his tongue out the side of his mouth, concentrating hard on his game. "You still aren't going to tell the wife, right?"

"Nope. But it might be a good idea to try running one of these days. Maybe even go for a walk?"

"I'm going to start on Monday." He laughed. "I see your Night Witch, and I'll raise you an electric Wizard. Take that!"

I assumed he was no longer talking to me, and I opened the garage. Inside, I grabbed a pint of railing touch-up paint, along with a paintbrush, scrubber, bucket of water, tarp, and a Snickers bar from Mr. Nguyen's not-so-secret stash. I went to the upstairs walkway, laid out the tarp, and removed the lid from the can, careful not to get paint on my blue Converses.

The railings weren't as bad as I thought. A few rust spots and splatters of bird poop. I dipped the brush in and cleaned off the excess paint along the side of the can.

Apartment 15's door jerked open behind me, and I turned around. Shanna poked her head out. "Are you here to collect rent?" she asked.

I looked at the paintbrush in my hand then back at her. "No."

"OK, cool. That's cool." Shanna's dark hair was pulled into a messy bun. Her eyes were cradled above dark purplish circles, and her face was flushed. "Can you tell me what my rent is?"

"Your rent? I don't remember the exact amount off the top of my head, but it's…the…same…as last…month." I sneezed. "Wow, excuse me." I rubbed my nose on my shoulder, feeling another sneeze coming on.

"Don't worry. It's cool. I'll check my lease." She drummed her fingers along the doorframe. "Can I get a copy of my lease?"

"You can come to the office later today and get a…copy…" I sneezed again.

"OK. Cool. I'll do that."

I sniffled. "How did your audition go?"

She gave me a look. "Audition?"

"You said last night that you had an audition today and were worried about smoke in your lungs?"

"Oh yeah, yeah, no. I didn't get it."

"I'm sorry."

"Yeah, it's cool…um…I'll drop rent later." She closed the door and locked it.

I sneezed one more time and cleared my scratchy throat. Allergies, or I was getting sick, which wouldn't be an ideal way to spend my birthday, but I guess painting rust and chiseling off bird poop wasn't exactly living it up either.

*Achoo!*

\* \* \*

Two hours later, and the railings were done. It was a tedious project that slightly improved the overall esthetic of the place. I was pleased.

The sound of high heels clicking against the pavement came from below and caught my attention. I peeked through the railings. Right on time, it was the brunette in tight pants who visited Apartment 23 every day at exactly 11:15 AM. She strutted down the sidewalk, swaying her hips as if she were walking a runway in Milan, not the sidewalk of a low-to-middle-class apartment complex in LA. When she reached the stairs, she turned sideways and took each step with her arms out to the side to help her balance. Her tight pants offered limited leg movement. It was comical to watch.

Ten minutes later the brunette made it to the top of the stairs. She continued her strut to Apartment 23 and knocked on the door to the tune of "Shave and a Haircut (Two Bits)." Trent answered and greeted her with an open-mouth kiss, as he usually did. He pulled her inside the apartment and closed the door behind them. This had been going on for the last three weeks, and I suspected Trent's wife, Alexis, had no idea.

As a woman, I felt it my duty to tell Alexis.

As the apartment manager, I felt it my duty to keep my mouth shut. Inserting myself into someone else's marriage was not only unprofessional but also stupid.

Very, very stupid.

And I was trying this new thing where I didn't do stupid things. So I minded my own business.

My phone buzzed from my back pocket, and I stumbled around, unsure what to do with the wet paintbrush and paint can in my hands. I'd ditched the tarp an hour before. It had been slowing me down. I balanced the paintbrush on the can and grabbed my phone. The screen said it was Tom.

"Happy birthday, Cam." I could hear the courthouse chatter in the background.

"Thanks. You're the first person besides my parents to wish me a happy birthday today."

"It's past eleven."

"What can I say? I'm popular." I sat back against the wall and crossed my legs. "What are you working on today?"

"A man wrongfully accused of hiring a hit man to kill his boss."

"Yikes. What's the sentence for something like that?"

"It doesn't matter. We're not losing…and it's twenty-five to life. But that's not why I called. What are you doing today?"

"The usual. Filing insurance claims, collecting rent, cleaning, watching television…are you laughing at me?"

"That's no way to spend a birthday. I'm taking you out."

*Out?* I glanced down at the phone to be sure I was, in fact, talking to Tom. We didn't go *out*. We exchanged playful banter and co-parented, but that was it. The last time we'd gone out, I got knocked up. "Do you mean you, me, and Lilly?"

"Just you and me," he said.

"Oh, I don't know…" I started to say, when the squeaky pool gate opened and slammed shut. I peeked through the railing. Chase and his partner, Hampton, walked through the breezeway side by side. Hampton was about two inches shorter and twelve inches wider than Chase, with no hair and wire-rimmed glasses. The office was closed, which meant the two had snuck in behind a car.

Oh geez.

Tom in my ear. Chase here. Suddenly, I couldn't have one without the other showing up.

Tom was still talking. Something about dinner, but I wasn't paying attention because Chase and Hampton stopped at Amy's apartment and knocked on the door.

"Sound like a plan?" Tom asked.

Chase kicked at the welcome mat while they waited. Hampton grabbed the note I'd left for Amy and read it. He handed it to Chase, he read it, they nodded to each other, and Chase shoved it back into the door.

"Cam!" Tom yelled to get my attention.

"Yeah, sorry." I switched the phone to my other ear. "*Um*…what?"

"I'll pick you up at 6:30 sharp."

Hampton cupped his eyes and peeked through Amy's window, but the blinds were still drawn.

"Cam? You there?"

"Yes…sorry. Sure, 6:30." I slid against the wall to become invisible.

*Are they here to question Amy about Jessica Wilders?*

Dumb question. Of course they were here to talk about Jessica Wilders. Amy didn't know anything, and she wasn't involved. Of this, I was sure. Yes, she didn't like Jessica. But she was far too passive-aggressive to do something so obvious as shoot her. If it were poison over a long period of time, I may have taken pause.

Amy was in the process of negotiating a two-season contract. This was huge. A permanent role on a hit show was her version of a golf cart. It was why we moved to LA. Well, why she moved to LA. I tagged along because that was what I did. I was a tagalong-er. If the network thought she was a person of interest, she'd be done. Fired. Back to a life of crappy hemorrhoid commercials—pun intended.

"Cam!"

"Sorry, Tom…" I bit at my lip. "Two detectives are here knocking on Amy's door. Do you think she's in trouble?"

"By 'detective,' do you mean Chase?"

"Does it matter?" I asked.

"Guess not. And no, it's standard for the police to interview anyone who spent time with the victim. I wouldn't read too much into it."

I heaved a sigh of relief. "You're probably right."

"Can you say that again?"

"No."

"I'm not hanging up until you say it."

"Fine. You're *probably* right."

"Thank you." I could hear the smile in his voice. "I'll be there to pick you up at 6:30."

I promised him I'd be ready on time and hung up the phone. Chase strolled toward the back walkway and stopped just below me. But before I could say anything, he pulled his phone from his pocket and slapped it to his ear.

"What'd you find out?" Chase said in lieu of a hello.

I rose to my feet. My toe tipped the can of paint, and a dribble fell and landed on the top of Chase's head. *Ahhhh!* I dropped into a push-up position. I imagined Chase touching the top of his head and looking up, but I didn't hear him say anything, so I stayed put. My muscles hurt, but it provided the anonymity to better eavesdrop. I caught every few words. "You ran a check on Michael Smith…right…I'm here now…let me handle it…no, I've got it…wait, I'll be right there…"

Chase bolted out to the carports, passed Amy's car without a second glance, and disappeared. Hampton trailed behind.

Michael Smith.
*Why does the name sound familiar?*

# CHAPTER FIVE

————

*See also: Graphologist*

As soon as I returned to the office, I did a search in our rental program for Michael Smith in both our current and past occupants. There were plenty of Michaels, plenty of Smiths, but no Michael Smith. I did a Google search and determined Michael Smith was a professional clogger in Maryland, and an artist in Canada, and a futbol player in Argentina, and a hiker gone missing six years ago, and a ten-year-old who'd won a spelling bee in Arkansas.

In short, my investigation was inconclusive, and I determined it time to put mission *Who is Michael Smith?* on the back burner and get to work.

Kevin was there. He'd come over to… I wasn't sure why he came over, but he was there, sitting in a swivel chair on the other side of my desk. For my birthday, Chase had had lunch delivered from my favorite sushi restaurant along with a warm butter cake from Mastro's Steakhouse. The man knew me well.

Kevin and I ate sushi while he read a magazine and I entered rent. It was *normal*. Pleasant, even. Not an adjective I'd associate with Kevin's name prior to his arrest. How far we'd come.

"Look at this for me." I showed Kevin a money order written in what looked like a heartbeat with no apartment number on it. This happened all the time. I'd get money orders with no name. No apartment number. Scribbled writing. The receipt still attached. Residents had way too much confidence in my psychic abilities. It would be flattering if it weren't so annoying. Especially the day before the trustee's visit. It would be nice to have all rent accounted for. "What do you think this says?" I asked.

Kevin lowered the magazine. "Looks like drunk writing."

"Or someone was in a hurry." But probably drunk.

Based on the amount, it belonged to a one-bedroom. I set it aside for now and stabbed a California Roll with my chopstick.

Kevin helped himself to a rainbow roll. "How long are you gonna keep that urn on your desk?" He pointed his sticks to *Mom*.

"I'll give the resident until Friday to call me back." I decided on the spot. "It's only been about twenty-four hours."

"Then what?"

I shrugged. "To be honest, I don't know."

*Note to self: check if local mortuary has a lost and found.*

"If I were you, I'd ditch it ASAP. Keeping it will cause bad luck," said Kevin.

"I don't believe in that stuff."

Kevin scooped up a spicy tuna roll. "That's what Lola said last week, and now this week she's dead."

"Lola isn't dead. Jessica Wilders is dead."

"Same difference. Jessica Wilders played Lola. She can't play Lola anymore. So both Jessica and Lola are dead. Double homicide."

"I don't think that's how it works."

"It should. Now I'll never know what happened between Frank and Lola. Can there even be a Frank with no Lola? The show is nothing without Frank." Kevin let out a harsh breath. "I don't know if I can keep watching."

"I'm sorry for your loss. How do you know so much about the show anyway? Did you have cable in prison?" My knowledge of the penitentiary system was limited. I watched a lot of crime shows, but I'd yet to get into prison dramas. There are only so many hours in the day.

"You get basic cable when you're good," he said.

"Huh. I didn't know that."

Learn something new every day.

I pushed against the desk and rolled to my apartment door. Lilly was asleep on the couch with her pink sweater on and Mickey Mouse tucked under her arm. She'd been fighting slumber since I'd picked her up from Mrs. Nguyen's, and finally she'd succumbed.

"Doesn't the chick in Apartment 36 work on *Ghost Confidential*?" Kevin asked from behind his magazine. A tabloid I'd never heard of—*Daily C-Leb Mag*.

I rolled back to my desk. "She plays a medium. Why?"

"Aren't you good friends with her?"

"I am, why?"

"Are the rumors true that she and Jessica were mortal enemies?"

"I wouldn't say mortal. They didn't get along, why?"

Kevin lifted the magazine. "There's an article in here about Jessica Wilders."

"Does it mention Amy's name?"

Kevin flipped another page and squinted at the writing. "No. Why?"

"Does it mention Michael Smith?"

Another flip. Another squint. "No. Why?"

"What about—"

He tossed the magazine across the desk.

*Guess I'll look for myself.*

On the cover was a candid photo of Jessica Wilders. She had on a red duster cardigan and furry boots. A security guard had her by the elbow, escorting her to a black SUV with black tinted windows. Her sleeves were pulled down over her hands, and her face was bare of makeup. Something about the picture had me unsettled. Specifically, Jessica's makeup-less face. There was something about her brown eyes that felt oddly familiar.

I opened the magazine and flipped past ten drug advertisements to the press release.

*Jessica Wilders, known for her starring role as Lola Darling on the hit television series* Ghost Confidential, *was discovered dead early Tuesday afternoon at her Malibu home. She was 28.*

*According to* TMZ, *Wilders' assistant found the actress after she failed to show up to a spa appointment. It's unclear if this was the work of an intruder or an inside job. Early reports suggest Wilders was shot multiple times. We will update as details are released.*

*Jessica Wilders is remembered for her television roles and her love of animals. Wilders worked campaigning for animal rights and co-founded the Animal Center for Chance in Los Angeles, a center for pets considered un-adoptable. In an interview on Ellen in 2016, Wilders made a reference to her childhood, saying, "It was taxing, but it was the love of animals that got me through it. Now look at me!"*

*At this time, police are following up on leads, but have yet to name a suspect or make an arrest.*

A gnawing feeling formed in the pit of my stomach.

The lobby door chimed. It was Sophie and her little boy Lumber from Apartment 38. She greeted me with a gummy smile and tucked a strand of dark hair behind her heavily pierced ear. "Hey, Cambria and…*Kevin*. I didn't know you were back."

Kevin grabbed his magazine and hid behind it.

I met them at the counter. Little Lumber had on a ninja costume, complete with eye mask and a utility belt. He had one finger looped in the belt, ready to fire a ninja star, and another finger fooling around with his nose.

"What can I do for you?" I handed Lumber a tissue. He made confetti with it, slashing sound effects and all.

"I brought you a birthday present." Sophie placed a gift bag on the counter and slid it towards me.

"Really?" I squeaked, feeling both touched and embarrassed. "How'd you know it was my birthday?"

"Silvia Kravitz told me."

"Oh." Made sense. She was the mayor.

Inside the bag was a dark purple button-up shirt with an oval cutout in the back. It was cute. I didn't own anything purple—wasn't sure the color looked good on me. "Thank you so much for this, Sophie. It's so…attractive."

She beamed. "I have to confess. I ordered it for me, but it was too big, and I thought it would look great on you."

Kevin coughed to cover a laugh.

Sophie's eyes went wide. "Oh no. I didn't mean it like *that*... It's just because I lost all this weight...and I'm short, and you're tall-ish."

She was an awkward gift giver. I was an awkward gift receiver. It worked.

"There's more in there!" she said in a panic. "On the bottom."

I pulled out a small bottle with a handwritten label— *Unbend*. "It's an essential-oil blend. This one helps with stress," she said. "You can rub it on your temples, or the back of your head. I like to use it in a diffuser. It's much safer than a wax melt." She jerked her head toward the lobby. "And foolproof."

*Sigh.*

I flipped open the lid and took a whiff. The scent traveled up my septum and encased me in a soothing floral, woodsy scent. Reminded me of Tom. "This is wonderful." I took another whiff and immediately pictured Tom standing in a field of lavender with nothing but his underpants on.

Mmmmm.

*Get a grip, woman.*

Sophie looked pleased. Lumber looked bored. He grabbed a brochure advertising our *Spacious One-Bedroom Apartments* from the counter and took a bite out of it. I was too *Unbend* to care.

"If you want more, I make these blends myself. I love them. Helps calm Lumber down."

The kid threw a crumpled brochure at my head.

"You'll have to give me more information." *Crap. Why did I say that?* Doing business with a resident was a terrible idea—awful, horrible, deadly.

Unless that resident was selling Girl Scout Cookies.

Then it was OK.

Well prepared, Sophie slapped the oil brochure on the counter.

My eyeballs nearly jumped out of my head. The little bottles cost thirty-five dollars! "Holy hell. Are they infused with Prozac?" *Oops.* Didn't mean to say that out loud.

"I...I could make that blend if you want. You can see the available ingredients here." She placed a chipped fingernail over the ingredients list. "I only just started making them."

Kevin didn't even attempt to hide his laugh this time.

"I'll look it over," I said.

Lumber threw another crumpled brochure at me. I swatted it away before it hit my face.

Sophie pulled a spray bottle from her purse and spritzed the air above Lumber's head. "Calm, baby!" she sang. "Inhale the peaceful scent, dammit!"

"No!" Lumber stomped his foot. "Stop, Mom!"

I didn't blame him. The "peaceful scent" smelled like feet. He flung a plastic ninja star at her nose and ran out the door.

Sophie sprinted after him. Though the window, I watched her chase Lumber, still frantically spritzing her oils. He made it all the way to the pool gate before she was able to catch him.

Kevin nearly fell out of his chair from laughing so hard.

"You're terrible." I sat down behind my desk with the gift bag.

"It's too big—I thought it would fit you!" He slapped his knee.

"Glad you're entertained."

He wiped his eyes. "Is today even your birthday?"

"Sure is." I held the shirt up to my chest. *Yeah, that's gonna fit.*

Kevin gave me a curious look. "You're twenty-nine, right?"

"Yes," I said slowly. "Why?"

He slammed a hand on the desk, and I jumped.

"Still got it!"

"Still got what?" I asked, utterly confused.

"I have a gift." Kevin tapped his temple with his forefinger. "I can figure out people's age and weight by looking at them. I've been doing it since I was a kid. Drove my mother nuts."

*I wonder why.*

"Let me guess your weight." He bounced around on the chair like a kid waiting for dessert.

"No thanks."

"Come on."

"Not a chance."

"It'll be my birthday present to you."

"I own a scale."

"It's your birthday?" came Lilly's sweet voice from the doorway.

Kevin and I spun around. She rubbed her red, sleep-crusted little eyes with her fist.

"It sure is. Come here." Lilly curled up on my lap, and I kissed her sweaty head. "Did you have a good nap?"

She nodded and nuzzled into my chest. "Daddy has something planned for your birthday."

"One hundred and thirty-eight pounds!" Kevin gave a victorious smile and threw his arms up in the air.

I looked at him, horrified. "No!"

*Yeeeessss.*

"He told me all about it last night," Lilly said, still nestled in my arms.

"He did?" I asked, feeling both surprised and annoyed. It wasn't a good idea to tell our daughter we were going out. As a matter of fact, it was terrible, awful, deadly! Well, maybe not deadly. But stupid.

Why would he say anything to her? That was mean. Get her hopes up, have her convinced her parents were going to be together, only to have them crushed when her commitment-phobic father freaked and ran (as he usually did).

"You're going out with the lawyer?" Kevin leaned back in the chair and put his hands behind his head. "I thought you were dating the cop."

"Shhh." I covered Lilly's ears. She knew Chase, and the two had a great relationship, but she didn't know he and I were in a semi-committed relationship. Unlike Tom, I didn't tell Lilly about my romantic ventures. Mostly because I didn't have many. Until recently.

"Mom, you're dating a cop?" Lilly asked with a confused tilt of her head. "You can't date a cop because Daddy has a big surprise for you."

I mentally slapped my forehead. Then I mentally slapped Kevin. And Tom.

"You don't need to worry about it, sweetie."

"Yah-ha. Daddy worked really hards on it. He said it was a *very* special *big* surprise and I'm not allowed to tell you."

A surprise? Tom and I didn't do *surprise*.

But we didn't go *out* either.

When Tom said he'd take me to dinner, he sounded casual, as if it was an after thought. Like, *Hey, I don't have anything better going on tonight. Let's hang.*

When I'd told Tom I was pregnant, he immediately shoved me into the friend zone. I referred to it as the Alcatraz zone, escapable only by death. Over the last six months, he'd thrown me several life rafts (a lingering touch, a flirty goodbye, a peck on the cheek) but had yet to make an actual move. Was tonight the night?

Oh geez.

I wasn't the type of gal who had more than one guy interested in her. I wasn't typically the type of gal who had *one* guy interested in her. I was the type of gal who sat on the couch in her sweats, eating ice cream straight out of the carton on a Friday night, by herself. If this weren't a no-pet property and I wasn't allergic to most things with fur, I'd have at least five cats.

Maybe ten.

I had no idea what to make of Tom planning a surprise for my birthday.

Of course, my source was a three-year-old.

But still. The kid was sharper than any three-year-old I'd met.

I was so confused.

This was right about when I'd call Amy. She'd help me overthink the situation. I sent her a quick text but got no reply. I suppose murder trumps my baby daddy troubles.

The uneasy feeling returned to my stomach.

*Gah, I really hope it isn't the sushi.*

# CHAPTER SIX

———

*See also: Alibi*

Because it was my birthday, and because the noise of the hydroxyl machine gave me a headache, and because Mr. Nguyen had to turn off the power to rewire the lobby, Patrick permitted me to close early for the day. Now I had plenty of time to get ready for my dinner with Tom and to call my mom back.

She immediately asked, "What's wrong?"

"Nothing!"

"If you tell me, I promise not to judge."

"Nothing is wrong, Mom." I was in the bathroom with my phone on speaker. Every piece of makeup I owned was on the counter, and the flat iron I'd had since high school was plugged in and set to *Max*.

I decided on the purple top Sophie had given me. It fit like a glove and, even better, looked good (if I do say so myself). It hugged my curves, and the opening in the back was so risqué, I felt quite naughty.

Granted, this was coming from a person who wears Mossimo T-shirts on the daily.

"Cambria, something is wrong. I can hear it in your voice."

Mom was relentless. She worked as a secretary at a busy meat-packing company in Fresno, and I could overhear the machines in the background. All the warehouse guys were afraid of her.

"Does it have to do with Jessica Wilders? Is Amy OK?"

"I haven't spoken to her yet."

"Why haven't you spoken to Amy? You two haven't gone more than a few hours without talking since the third grade. Did you get in a fight?"

"No, she's…not allowed to talk about it right now." I hoped I was right about that. It was getting harder to keep the worst-case-scenario portion of my brain quiet though.

"Is that why you're so upset?"

"I'm not upset, Mom." I leaned over the counter and applied a thin layer of eyeliner. "What's new with you?"

"Nothing. I called you this morning, and you didn't pick up."

I could hear her eyes rolling.

"That's because I was sleeping." I leaned back to check out my eyeliner skills—which were lacking. One side was thin. The other looked like I'd used a crayon.

"Anyway, happy birthday…something is wrong. What is it? Work?"

"No." I wiped the liner off and mascara'd my lashes. "Work is good."

"Is it a boy?" Her voice took on a curious tone. Here we go. "You're way too young and far too pretty with way too much potential to still be single. You should get out more."

"I get out," I said, feeling defensive. "Sometimes."

"Just tell me what's wrong."

"I'm fine."

"Sweetheart, I'm your mother, and I can tell when something is wrong."

I strangled my phone.

To the rescue, Lilly shuffled in with my black heels on and struck a little teapot pose. "You talking to Grammie?"

"Yes, here." I took the phone off speaker and handed it to her.

"*Chào bạn.*" Lilly shuffled back into my closet in search of a matching handbag.

I returned to preening.

Einstein tamed. Teeth brushed. Cheeks blushed. Deodorant applied—twice because I sweated *a lot* when I was nervous. And when I'm excited. And when I'm hot. And when I'm breathing.

Done.

Now it was time to practice my surprised face, in case Lilly was right and Tom did have a surprise for me. When I was genuinely surprised, I looked constipated. When I knew I was about to be surprised, I could provide a better reaction.

I stared at my reflection in the mirror and opened my mouth wide. It looked like I was preparing for a dental exam.

Not good.

Moving on. I placed my hand on my chest and gasped.

Even worse.

Suddenly, Amy's reflection joined mine in the mirror, and I stumbled back. "Hey, what are you—"

Amy pressed her finger to my lips and *shhhh'd* me.

She mouthed, *Who is Lilly talking to?*

*My mom*, I mouthed back, unsure of why we were silently conversing. Then I took her in—the leggings, sport bra, and loose-fitting tee. Her blonde and green streaked hair shoved into a trucker's hat, her makeup-less face fraught with distress.

Amy dropped her hand. "Why are you so dressed up?"

I stared at her in disbelief.

"Oh no. I'm the worst friend ever." She brought her hand to her mouth—looking more authentically surprised than I ever could. "It's just…it's just…" Her breathing became quicker and quicker. "Someone is trying to frame me for the Jessica Wilders murder, and I'm kinda freaking out about it. I'm so sorry. I totally forgot today was your birthday."'

I wasn't sure how to respond, so I said "Ummmmm" until my brain could think of something better.

Amy sat on the toilet seat and bit at her nail bed, a habit she'd kicked in high school. And her forehead was crinkled, a habit she'd kicked when we moved to LA. You know—wrinkles.

"Hold on…" My brain spun. "Is this real? You seriously think you're being framed?"

"Yes!" Amy was now up and pacing the length of my bathroom, twirling a loose tendril of hair between her fingers. I slid one butt cheek onto the counter, to give her more pacing space. My bathroom wasn't that big.

"Tell me what happened?" I said calmly.

Amy had a tendency to be overdramatic. As did I, but I typically kept mine in my head, while she made ordering a pizza sound like a dire situation.

"OK, so..." She paused to chew off her cuticle and spit it out. "On Monday afternoon, I got a call from *the* EJ Ryder."

"Who?"

She stopped pacing long enough to gape at me. "The major television producer."

I shrugged. No idea.

"She created that show you love, *If Only*."

"Oh. I do love that show." It was about a woman who was on the hunt to find her late husband's killer but ended up falling for the lead detective on the case. Just when things heated up between them, the husband returned and she had to choose between the father of her children and her lover. I never missed an episode. "Right. EJ Ryder contacted you, and..."

"So when EJ Ryder wants a meeting, you take it. The thing is, you know we're negotiating my contract with *Ghost Confidential*, and if they found out I was meeting with EJ Ryder, they'd totally write me off. So I don't tell anyone I'm meeting with her. Like, anyone. Not even my agent. I get to the place—it's a studio in Culver City, a small one, but whatever. The thing is, it was closed. So I wait, and wait, and wait, and no one ever showed up! I was there for almost two hours waiting like a total idiot, pulling at the doors and knocking."

"Are you sure you had the right place?"

"Positive. And I couldn't call EJ's assistant back because she'd called from a blocked number. So I waited until yesterday morning to call her office, and I left a message. Later in the day, after I talked to you, the assistant's assistant called me back and said EJ's been out of town for the past two weeks, and she'd never planned to meet me, and no one had called me to set up a meeting. Then I heard about Jessica and how the cops were questioning everyone on the set today. They said Jessica was killed between eight and ten on Monday night. And I realized at that same time, I was waiting in an empty parking lot by myself with zero alibis. So I called in sick and stayed home so I could figure it out."

The timing was fishy. I'd give her that. "Why don't you pull up your phone records and show the police you had a call from a private number to corroborate your story? Did you tell Spencer about all this? What did he say?"

By the look on her face, telling him hadn't occurred to her. "I told him when I got home where I was because he asked. I didn't tell him that your boyfriend was pounding on my door today, demanding to speak to me."

"He didn't *pound* on your door. He knocked. If anything, you not answering makes you look guilty. Plus, he bolted out of here. I think they might have a lead now, and maybe he doesn't even need to speak with you anymore. Why don't you call him?"

"And say what?"

"The truth?"

She looked at me as if I'd lost my mind and said, "You've lost your mind. I can't say that. I'll sound crazy. I can't be seen at any police station right now either, and there's no way I'm telling anyone where I was. I'll lose my job. What if I say you and I were together Monday night?"

I had to stop and think about what I did Monday night. When you have no life, it's hard to differentiate one day from the next. *Let me think…* I must have been home watching *If Only*. "Nope, won't work. Chase stopped by for a few hours Monday night after Lilly went to bed. What if this person who called you is the same person who killed Jessica? A crazed fan that is targeting stars of the show? Think about it. They sent you to a vacant parking lot at night?"

"That really helps me feel better. *Thanks*."

I knelt down in front of her. "Maybe you misunderstood the assistant? You weren't meant to meet EJ Ryder, but someone else?"

"I thought about that, but then…" Amy made a face.

I knew that face. Nothing good came after that face.

"Oh no. What happened?"

She was up and pacing again. I was sure she'd met her daily step goal by now.

"So you know how I love smoothies in the morning?"

"Yes, and?"

"This morning I was making my smoothie and heating up my face bag. It's this new thing you put on your face to help with morning puffiness—"

"Yeah, yeah, get to the *more*."

"I spilled my smoothie on my shirt, so I ran to my car to get stain remover, 'cause I'd just bought some."

"You're killing me! Get to the point."

Amy pulled a key ring from her back pocket and handed it to me. "One of those keys is to Jessica's house," she said. "Someone planted it in my car."

*Ahhh!* I dropped it on the ground. "Why'd you hand it to me?"

"So you could see it!"

"How do you know it's a key to her house?"

Amy was frantic. "Because look at it. It has her address and gate code on the tag!" she screamed. "I think these are her assistant's keys!"

"How do you know?"

"Because it has her assistant's name on it!"

"I thought you wanted to keep quiet?"

"I do!"

"Then stop yelling at me!"

"Oh." She covered her mouth. "Sorry," she whispered.

I bent down and examined the keys. Attached to the metal ring was a black Toyota car key, a metal circle with *Z* stamped on it, a house key, and a keychain tag, the same brand I used to label apartment keys. On one side, *Gate code: 9876* was written. I flipped the tag over, using an eyeliner pencil—*1164 Malibu Way.*

Crap.

I looked up at her. "Are you sure this is to Jessica's house?"

"Yes! On Monday, Jessica's assistant, Zahra, was asking everyone if they'd seen her keys. She said they were missing from her purse. I didn't think anything of it. I lose my keys all the time. But now…crap! Cambria, the keys were on the backseat of my car. Now it looks like I took Zahra's keys so I could get access to Jessica!" She clawed at her neck. "You've read about this, right? What they're saying in the press? They've already named me a suspect, and now this!"

"Who is 'they'?"

"Everyone! TMZ, C-Leb Mag, a new blogger named Dirty Dan who is smearing me online. It's awful, Cambria."

I pulled the flat iron plug from the wall. "Leave the keys. Let's go comb the internet for information."

Lilly had hung up with my mom and was now on the bed, watching Netflix on my phone. Which meant she'd be occupied for the next three days if I left her alone.

I sat behind my desk and googled "Jessica Wilders and Amy Montgomery" while Amy paced. At the top of my search was a news article written an hour ago titled, *Vicious On-Set Fight the Day before Jessica Wilders Found Dead.*

I clicked on the website and scanned the article. "Amy! This says you called Jessica a gapped-tooth troll?"

"Because she kept fumbling her lines and blaming me for it. She called me an amateur. I wouldn't have called her a troll if I knew she'd end up dead the next day."

I continued to read. "Did you throw your kale smoothie at her?"

"I didn't *throw* it at her. It fell out of my hand and…landed on her. She was on edge all day, snapping at everyone. I couldn't take it anymore."

Well, crap.

I went back to Google and clicked on the next article, posted an hour ago by Dirty Dan.

*Top Ten Reasons Why I Think Amy Montgomery Killed Jessica Wilders.*

"Oh no."

"What?" Amy demanded. "Tell me."

"Nothing." I tilted the screen away from her.

"Not nothing. I can tell by your face!" Amy gave me a hard shove, and I rolled to the window. "Ahhhh! They made a top-ten list! I told you…the public…jury…has already…convicted…me!" Her breathing quickened.

I grabbed a paper bag and shoved it over her mouth. "Breath," I said. "Calm down and just breathe."

"Why...does...this...bag...smell...like...fish?" she asked between breaths.

"Sushi for lunch. Keep breathing."

There was a knock on the door. I thought Amy was going to faint. "It's the feds!" she cried. I shoved the bag back over her mouth.

"It's probably a resident," I assured her. "Keep breathing."

Amy followed me to the door, inflating and deflating the bag. I placed my eye up to the peephole and—crud.

OK, so maybe she was right.

# CHAPTER SEVEN

———

*See also: Accomplice*

"It's the police," I whispered to Amy, trying to keep my cool.

She fell against the wall like she'd been shot in the chest. I told her to stay put and opened the door enough to shove my head out. Standing in front of me was Chase, wearing the same suit as earlier, though his tie was pulled loose. Hampton was behind him. His tie was always pulled loose. I was sure Hampton had a first name, but Chase called him Hampton, so I did too.

"Hi, how may I help you?" I smiled in what I hoped was not an I-may-or-may-not-have-a-person-of-interest-hiding-behind-my-door kind of way.

Chase narrowed his eyes. "Can we come in?"

"Inside my house?" Crap. Crap. Crap. "Errrrr…no. Lilly is asleep."

"Momma, your phone isn't working! There's the spinning thing!" Lilly hollered from the bedroom.

I reached my foot back and kicked the router on the television stand. "Never mind. It works now."

"Sleep talker that one." I chuckled. "Um, sorry, I'm not…decent."

"That's fine with me." The corner of Chase's mouth twitched upward. "I'll come in, and Hampton can stay out here." He took a step toward me.

I put a hand out to stop him. "I mean, I'm not decent because…it's…personal. I'm having personal problems. Women's problems."

Chase studied me, and I squirmed, refusing to make eye contact. "Have you spoken to Amy today?"

*Oh hell.*

An episode of *If Only* came to my head. A dialogue between the lead character, Bobbie Dart, and Detective Russell, about successfully lying to the cops. Don't pause, don't talk too fast, don't give out too much information, no hand motions, and stick as close to the facts as possible so you don't trip on your words.

Of course, on the show, the cop in question wasn't a romantic interest.

I looked straight into Chase's eyes and kept my hands still. He had beautiful eyeballs. Bright green with specs of gray… *Concentrate, woman!* "Yes. I have spoken with Amy today."

Chase scratched his chin without breaking eye contact. "Her neighbor said she might be with you."

*Yeah, OK, I can't do this.*

"Can you hold on one moment? I…have…to…um…pee." I closed the door carefully, feeling all shaky. Amy had assumed a fetal position. "He wants to come in," I whispered to her. "I think he knows you're here."

Amy looked up at me with a helpless expression and shook her head. *Make him go away,* she mouthed.

"I can't."

"Please, please, Cambria. I can't do this right now," she whispered. "I have to come up with a better plan before I talk to them."

"This is a terrible idea. You look guilty when you avoid the cops."

"Please." She was on the verge of tears, and I broke.

"Fine," I hissed through gritted teeth. "Don't make any noise." I swallowed a few times. Took a few breaths. Pulled what I hoped was a poker face, and reopened the door. I promptly shifted my eyes to Chase's feet. He had on black shoes with scuffmarks on the right toe. "I'm not sure where Amy is now," I said.

Chase shifted his weight to his heels.

"Has she ever talked about her relationship with Jessica Wilders?" Hampton asked.

I didn't have to look to know Amy was on the cusp of a nervous breakdown. I heard the sushi bag crinkle at a more rapid pace. "I think they had mutual respect as actors."

"Do you know why she didn't come to work today?" Chase asked.

"I think she's a bit freaked out about Jessica's death."

"Could you call Amy and see where she is?" Chase asked.

"No. If you want to talk to her, then you can call her yourself. She's my best friend, and I can't be in the middle of this." Even though, technically speaking, I was in the middle of the two of them. Quite literally.

Chase and Hampton shared a look, and I had a feeling they weren't buying it.

"Please let her know we're looking for her," Chase said to me. "It's important. If I don't hear from her soon, we can put out an ATL."

"That means an attempt to locate," Hampton said.

"She knows what ATL means," Chase said to him. "She also knows what being an accessory is." He looked at me with those beautiful green eyes. "She watches a lot of cop shows."

If I wasn't mistaken, that was a threat. Chase was threatening me. If I weren't near a stroke, I might have been turned on.

"I will pass this on to her when I see her—if I do, which I probably won't because—I have a thing tonight. A—" *Stop talking, Cambria. Close your mouth and prohibit words from exiting before they arrest you.* "OK. I better go!" I closed the door. It bounced off Chase's shiny black shoe, leaving a new scuffmark.

*I may faint.*

"Hey, I haven't had the chance to talk to you." He smiled, flashing all his pearly whites at me. "Did you enjoy your lunch?"

"It was…pleasant."

"Are you sure there's nothing you want to say to me?"

"Thank you?"

He studied me, and I almost caved.

"Happy birthday, Cambria," he finally said.

*Oh hell.*

"Thanks," I managed. "You too." I closed the door and fell back against it.

That was painful.

Did I just say "you too"*?*

Smooth.

I beat the back of my head against the door.

"I told you I'm being framed." Amy wept from her spot on the floor.

"I just lied to Chase." I slapped my hands over my eyes. What was I thinking?

"So what? I lie to Spencer all the time." She put the bag up to her mouth and breathed.

"Your boyfriend is a dentist. Mine's a human lie detector. That's what. This isn't good." I went back to beating the back of my head against the door while Amy breathed into her bag.

We did this for a while until she blew a hole in the bottom of her bag and I got a headache.

"What am I supposed to do?" Amy finally asked with a whimper.

"You need a good lawyer." I rubbed my temples.

"Do you think Tom will represent me?"

The thought of Tom, Chase, and Amy all together in an interrogation room gave me indigestion.

"OK, here's an idea," I said. "What if you call Chase and tell him what happened? He's reasonable, and I'm sure he'll believe you. Wouldn't you rather give yourself up than be taken down to the station and questioned?"

"No. I will never, ever say what happened. Are you kidding me? I'll lose my job."

I let out a grunt. "You'll also lose your job if you're arrested."

Amy crossed her arms. "I'm not talking to the police yet. Not until I have a better plan."

I hung my aching head when another idea trotted into my mind. "What if we go to the studio and see if there are security cameras in the parking lot? If there are, that's your alibi. You don't have to say why you were at the studio. Just that you were. Or you could say it was in the name of character research. We'll see if they have cameras, tell Chase, and he can check the footage. Then by this time tomorrow, you're free and clear, and the network won't know anything about EJ Ryder, and the police can release a statement clearing your name."

Amy shook her head so fast, her face blurred.

"Hear me out." I scooted closer. "Someone made sure you were in an empty parking lot by yourself. Suddenly a key to Jessica's house is in your backseat. And the press has already pegged you a suspect."

"This is not making me feel better."

"Let me finish." I took her hands in mine. Her palms were clammy. "As I see it, one of two things will happen. You'll either be hunted down by Chase and taken to the station to be questioned. Or you'll give yourself up willingly. We'll stop at the studio to see about cameras. Then we'll call Tom and get his advice. Either way, you're going to have to come clean, tonight."

"But—" she started to say.

"I know. I know. You don't want the press to find out. But if we call Chase first, maybe he'll meet us at your apartment?"

"I mean—*but* it's your birthday," she said.

Oh, that. Happy freaking birthday to me.

"This is more important. Let me get Lilly." I started to stand, and Amy pulled me back down. "What now?"

"What about your big meeting tomorrow?" she asked.

"What about it?"

"Don't you need to get ready for it tonight?"

Amy had a doctorate in procrastination.

"I've got it all ready. Let's go." I pulled her to her feet.

# CHAPTER EIGHT

———

*See also: Just a girl standing in front of a zombie, trying not to faint*

Studio Bea's parking lot was big enough to fit six economy-sized cars if everyone agreed to enter and exit their car through the trunk. The lot sat in front of a large warehouse-sized building with black awnings and steel-framed doors. Two doors belonged to Studio Bea and the third to a business called Cadaver's Cavern. Only in Los Angeles could you find a store named after a corpse and not think twice of it.

You know, movie props.

The studio's windows were dark, but Cadaver's lights were on. I leaned over the steering wheel and read the sign mounted to the lamppost—*Tenant and Customer Parking Only. Violators Will Be Towed.* No mention of surveillance.

"Let's get out and have a look around. We'll talk to the Cadaver's people and see if they have cameras." I killed the engine and unbuckled my seat belt. Amy didn't move. She sat with one leg crossed over the other, hands folded, face in a pout. "You have to get out first. Then I go," I reminded her. We were in my car. The driver's side door was stuck shut and had been since an unfortunate meeting with a runaway dumpster.

Amy picked at the tape keeping my passenger seat together. "I shouldn't have called her a gap-toothed troll. I mean, she acted like one, but I shouldn't have said it. I'd never kill her though. What if I go to jail for a crime I didn't commit? Or—" She gasped. "What if my career is ruined and the only job I can get is on *Celebrity Tango*? I'd die!"

She would indeed. Beautiful, yes. Charming, always. Rhythm, none.

It was only slightly concerning she was more worried about doing reality TV than going to prison.

"Do you want this?" Lilly held up a grease-stained Taco Bell bag she found on the backseat. "You could blow in it?"

Amy took the offered bag and shoved it on her face. "Ugh. Does everything you have smell like fat?"

"Pretty much. Oh!" I remembered the oils. "I have something better than a bag." I pulled out the bottle of Unbend and paused. I ran through the list of ingredients in my head. Amy was allergic to nuts. I was pretty certain there weren't any, but before I could be sure, she yanked the bottle out of my hand, flipped the lid, and chugged.

"Ew, gross! What is this? Sour Vodka?"

I froze, with what I was sure was a face of horror. "You weren't supposed to drink it!"

She wiped her mouth with the back side of her hand. "What was I supposed to do with it?"

"Smell it, or rub it, or diffuse it. Why would I keep vodka in my bag?"

Amy shrugged. "If I had your job, I'd keep liquor on hand."

"What's vodka?" Lilly asked.

"It wasn't vodka. It was a homemade essential-oil blend one of my residents made." I grabbed the bottle from Amy and peered down into the empty vessel.

Amy fanned her mouth. "I can't feel my tongue."

"Your breath smells really good," Lilly said.

I had my phone out. "According to WebMD, you should be fine. But you may experience stomach cramps or vomiting. You should drink milk, or eat yogurt, or sour cream, or cheese, but don't drink water.'" I looked up. "Why are you drinking water? I just said not to!"

Amy showered the dashboard with $H_2O$. "My mouth is on fire!" She grabbed Lilly's pink canteen from the cup holder, and I swatted it out of her hand.

"It's almond milk!" I grabbed a container of fish crackers that was wedged between my seat and the console. "Eat these. It'll take the burn away."

"But *essss* carbs," she said with her tongue wagging.

"A handful of fish crackers isn't going to kill you."

"I'll wait for the burning to sssstop."

"So be it." We should all have such restraint. I tossed a few fish into my mouth and turned around to the backseat. "You take good care of Auntie Amy," I told Lilly. "I'll only be a minute."

"Why does hers look like a dog?" Lilly pointed to Amy's extended tongue.

"It's *she* looks like a dog," I corrected. Grammar was important. I turned to Amy. "Can I trust that you won't try to kill yourself while I'm gone?"

Amy gave a pitiful nod.

Good enough. I wasn't about to bring my child to a place called Cadaver's.

I climbed over Amy and out the door. After one lap around the small parking lot, I determined there to be no cameras. None visible anyway. I went to Cadaver's. Inside were shelves of skulls in every shape and size. Some had crushed craniums, others broken jaws. There was an entire section dedicated to intestines. Fake dead bodies were on racks with hooks in their backs so you could easily skim through them like you were at Nordstrom looking for a new sweater.

There was also an entire section of scented candles.

A guy named Jack, per the tag pinned to his suspender, was stocking the severed-foot section. He had a derby cap on his head, wing-tipped shoes on his feet, tight pants, a nice butt...*wow, I mean*...he was a good-looking gentleman. Reminded me of Clark Kent. Like he should be reporting from the *Planet*, not working with fake dead bodies.

"What can I do you for?" Jack tipped his hat.

I fanned my face. A wave of nausea slid through my stomach, and I went light-headed. There were a lot of limbs lying around.

*They're fake.*
*They're fake.*

*They're all fake.*

I gulped. "Hi. Do you know if they have cameras in the parking lot, by chance?"

Jack stood and looped his thumbs in his suspenders. "Nope. Property manager around here is too cheap."

*Ew.* It was a turnoff when anyone insulted his or her property manager. But I had to move past the blunder. "What about inside the store? Maybe one pointed toward the front?" The door and windows were tinted, but you could still see outside.

"Of course. There's a lot of money here."

I glanced at the eyeball section. *Blech.* "Good. Um, where exactly are they?"

Jack raised a brow. "Why? You planning on robbing the place?"

"No, no, nooo," I said. "Not at all. Sorry. I should have explained first. It's just that I'm not used to all these…corpses. Hey, that one looks familiar."

"Which one?"

"The one with the Elvis lip and bow tie over there on the rack." I pointed.

Jack followed my gaze. "He was on *Miami PD* fall finale. He'll be on *If Only* next week, if you watch for him."

"Really? I love that show!"

"This foot appears in Episode 217."

"Really? Whose foot? Wait…" *Concentrate, woman.* "Never mind. That's not why I'm here. I'm asking about the cameras because my friend was here Monday night around 9:00 PM and I need to prove it."

"We close at seven. Sorry. She couldn't have been here."

"She was in the parking lot. She was supposed to meet someone at the studio next door, but they never showed. Do you know if they have outside security cameras?"

"Nope. They closed down."

Oh no. "When did they close?"

Jack thought for a moment. "About a month ago? They moved the studio to Vegas. Fewer laws and taxes."

Crap. "Did EJ Ryder ever film there?"

Jack's eyebrows drew together. "EJ Ryder, the mega television producer?"

"Yes, that's the one. Did she ever film next door?"

Jack laughed. Not just a chuckle either, but a full-body someone-told-a-hilarious-joke-and-I-might-pee-my-pants-from-laughing-so-hard laugh. I took that as a no. "There's not a chance EJ Ryder would be caught dead at Studio Bea."

"Why not?"

"They filmed mostly adult material."

I blinked. "Porn?"

"Yep." Jack snapped his suspenders. "They had some big hits in their heyday."

This was getting worse by the minute. I could picture Amy banging on the door of an old porn studio, demanding to be let in. No doubt she was dressed in something skimpy—proudly displaying all her surgically enhanced assets.

If there were cameras, it would have gone viral by now.

"Can I see your security footage from Monday evening, from around 8:00 to 10:00 PM?" I asked. "My friend does this pacing thing when she's nervous, and she may have passed your door. Several times."

"No pro-blemo, my dear. The boss will be in tomorrow morning. He'll be happy to help you out," Jack said.

"Is there any way you could check the security footage for me right now?"

Jack was shaking his head before I even finished. "Chuck doesn't want people touching his equipment."

"What if we don't tell him?" I winked.

Jack leaned in. He had enough aftershave on to perfume a small nation. "You never told me your name."

"It's, um, Cambria."

"Well *Um Cambria*, that's a pretty name for a pretty girl."

*Is he...flirting with me?*

What an interesting place for a meet-cute.

I fought the urge to retort with a self-deprecating remark like—*are your eyeballs cadavers? ha-ha*—but chose to use his interest to my advantage. I stifled a sneeze, because sneezing isn't sexy, and seductively ran a hand through Einstein. My finger got caught in a tangle. I wrangled it out and took a chunk of hair with it.

Clearly, I wasn't going to seduce my way into Chuck's equipment. I tried a different approach and batted my baby blues. "Jack, my friend is in trouble, and if I could get the footage of her in the parking lot, it would potentially save an innocent person's life. Please help me out?"

Jack picked the box of feet off the ground. "Fine. Come with me to the back room, and I'll show you the setup."

Following a man who specialized in dead bodies to a back room didn't seem like a good idea.

But I did it anyway.

Except when Jack said they had a surveillance system, I was expecting one of those setups you see at Costco. This thing was straight out of an episode of *CSI: Cyber*. Let's not forget the array of all things death inside the office, plus a few Oscars, an Emmy, and various other awards. I sat down behind the screens and wiggled the mouse. It asked for a password, and I looked up at Jack.

"Crap," he said.

I typed in crap. Didn't work.

"I meant *crap*, I don't remember the password."

Oh. Obviously, Lilly inherited her keen intellect from her mom. Honestly.

*Good one, Cambria.*

In my defense, the surrounding limbs reduced my faculties. Gross.

Jack took the mouse from me and tried a few passwords while I excused myself to go call Tom. His voicemail answered after only one ring. "Tom, it's Cambria. I'm so sorry, but I don't think I'll make it home by 6:30, and, if I do, I can't go out tonight. Amy is in trouble. It's a long story. But we're going to see if the police can meet us at her apartment later. Could you call me when you get this, please? Or just come by. I think she's going to need legal counsel. OK, bye."

I walked back into the room and found Jack playing solitaire on the computer.

"No luck?" I asked.

"Sorry. We're going to have to wait for Chuck to get here."

Great. I reached into my bag and pulled out a business card, grabbed a pen from the desk, and wrote my cell number on it. "Here's my information. If by some chance Chuck returns tonight, could you call me?"

Jack took the card and looked it over. "You're a property manager?"

"I manage a building off Sepulveda."

"Really?" He flicked the card. "Interesting. That's a decent area."

"It is. We have a one-bedroom available, if you're interested." Was there ever a wrong time to rent an apartment?

I guess one could argue this moment wasn't right, being that my best friend was being framed for murder and I was surrounded by fake dead bodies. But I had one vacancy, and Jack appeared gainfully employed.

"I'll keep you in mind." Jack took out his wallet and slipped my card in. "What kind of trouble is your friend in?"

"The life-in-prison kind."

"She's lucky to have a friend looking after her."

"Agreed."

Jack walked me to the front. I kept my eyes straight ahead and away from the zombies in the corner.

*Guess I won't be sleeping tonight.*

I pushed open the door and left. Amy was right. Someone had gone through a great effort to be sure she was occupied during the murder, at a location she'd never reveal, without an alibi—and they had planted the keys in her car. We had to tell Chase before any real cadavers entered the picture.

I slowed as I approached my car. It was empty.

Lilly and Amy were gone.

# CHAPTER NINE

———

*See also: Nurse*

"Lilly!" I called out, turning around. "Amy! Where are you?" I pulled on the car handle. The door was unlocked, and Amy's phone was on the seat.

Panic clumped in my throat. She'd never leave her phone! "I'm such an idiot. Why do I think I'm a freaking detective? Why didn't I tell Chase that Amy was hiding behind my door, scared, and trust the process? Trust the system!"

I was about to call 9-1-1 when I heard Lilly shouting for me. I whirled around. Lilly and Amy walked down the dirt embankment, hand-in-hand. Lilly had a giant Slurpee, blue lips, and a smile of pure delight across her face. I barely registered Amy and ran to hug Lilly.

"Where were you? I nearly had a heart attack," I snapped at Amy.

She had her wallet clutched in her hand and a frog face on. That was what my grandma Ruthie used to say when any of us cousins were about to throw-up. *Why are you so frog-faced?*

"We walked to the gas station on the corner." Amy rubbed her stomach. "Lilly had to pee."

"Lilly had to pee," I repeated in horror. "You took my child into a gas station bathroom?" I rummaged through my bag, pulled out a package of wipes, and began de-germing Lilly. "Do you know what you can catch from a dirty bathroom? Streptococcus, Staphylococcus, *E. coli*, and shigella bacteria, hepatitis!" According to Lilly's pediatrician, I spent too much time on WebMD. Lilly held out her arms one at a time, still sipping her Slurpee, used to her neurotic mother.

"I washed her hands. She's fine." Amy leaned against the hood of my car and crossed her arms over her belly. "Did you ask about the cameras?"

I walked the pile of wipes to the trash can under the lamppost, dropped them in, and dusted off my hands. "Yes, I did. Here's the good news. They don't have cameras out here, but they have an impressive surveillance system inside the Cadaver's store."

Amy's mouth dropped open. "Why is that good news? I didn't go inside. They were closed."

"There's a good chance they got at least one shot of you outside the front door. Also, the studio has been closed for a month. Also, it's a porn studio. Also, you're right. Someone is trying to peg Jessica's murder on you. Also, it's time to call—"

"Don't say it."

"Avoiding the police is not going to end in your favor, Amy. Just tell Chase exactly what happened. Plus, they may already have a lead. Do you know a Michael Smith?"

"I know, like, seven Michael Smiths." She threw her hands up and paced. "We went to high school with one. What does that have to do with anything?"

*Ohhh!*

Right. Michael Smith. That was why the name sounded familiar. Last I'd heard he lived in Fresno and sold solar panels. Probably not the right Michael Smith.

Amy shoved her torso into my car and dug around in my glove compartment. "What are you doing?" I asked.

"I'm looking for a pen and paper." She pulled out a red crayon and a Verizon bill. "This will work." She laid the bill on the hood of my car.

"Do I even want to know what you're doing?"

"Thinking." Amy scribbled on the blank side. "Spencer does this. He writes out his thoughts. It helps him process faster. It's, like, a doctor thing."

"You realize you're not a doctor."

"Quiet! I'm thinking."

I tapped my foot. This was ridiculous, and I was growing impatient. "So what have you come up with so far?"

She didn't answer.

I read over her shoulder and rolled my eyes. "Mexico? You're going to flee to Mexico? That's what you've got?"

"We could go there and wait for this whole thing to blow over."

"What do you mean '*we*'?"

"Oh! Oh! Oh!" Lilly raised her hand. "I want to go to Mexico!"

"Not forever. Just like a spontaneous vacation," Amy said. "We'll say we had the trip planned and play dumb." Amy let out a moan, clutched her stomach, and folded in half. The hat on her head fell to the ground.

"There are way too many *we's* in that plan." I picked the hat up and tossed it into the car. "You can doodle all you want on a piece of paper, but you know the best thing to do is talk to the police. We both know that's what's going to end up happening. Let's get it over with."

Amy drew in a deep breath through her nose. "I can't go to jail."

"They have STDs there," Lilly offered, as if this were a good thing.

"Why don't you wait for us in the car?" I told her.

"Can I pretend to drive?"

"Go for it."

"Best day ever!" She climbed in and laid on the horn.

I placed a hand on Amy's bony back. "I know you're scared, but Jessica was murdered, and you may have knowledge that could help find the killer. I already left Tom a message to meet us at your apartment so you two can discuss your legal obligations."

The lamppost above us flickered on and reflected off Amy's nose piercing. I could now see just how frog-faced she was.

"Let's go." I slipped my hand around Amy's tiny waist. "You can lie down in the back seat, and we'll stop at the store and get something for your stomach."

"Like an Ativan?"

"I was thinking more along the lines of peppermint tea o Pepto-Bismol."

"Eh. My idea is better."

"You don't want to be loopy when you're interviewed by the police."

"I don't?"

"No." I was steering her to the car when a black sedan raced around the corner and screeched into the parking lot. Amy and I grabbed hold of each other and jumped up on the trunk of my car to avoid being hit. The sedan slid to a halt, positioning itself diagonally behind my car, blocking us in.

*OK, now I'm frog-faced, too.*

# CHAPTER TEN

─────

*See also: Interpreter*

Chase stepped out of the vehicle and slammed the door shut. I clutched my chest and waited for my heart to jump back on rhythm. If I didn't have a heart attack before I was thirty, it will be a miracle.

"How'd you find us?" I asked him. "Wait…did you put a tracker on my car?"

Chase gave me a look. "No. I'd never put a tracker on your car. We followed you."

"We?"

Hampton stepped around from the passenger side and adjusted his pants like he was a sheriff and this here was his town. "What are you ladies up to?"

Amy and I shared a glance. Lilly laid on the horn, and the two of us jumped off the trunk of my car, still holding on to each other.

Chase shook his head. "Someone better tell us what's going on, or I'll arrest you both."

"On what grounds?" I demanded.

"Obstruction of justice."

"OK!" I turned to Amy. "Are you going to tell them, or should I?"

Amy took a deep breath and grimaced. "If I talk too much, I'll barf."

"Fine." I distanced myself from Amy. "On Monday, Amy received a call from a blocked number by a woman claiming to be the assistant to EJ Ryder. EJ produces *If Only*." Chase despised the show, mostly because it appeared the protagonist would end up with the baby daddy, not the cop. "The assistant told Amy to meet EJ Ryder here. But when Amy got here, both the studio and Cadaver's Caverns were closed. She waited around for a few hours then went home. When she heard about Jessica Wilders' murder, she was concerned because she had no alibi. We stopped here to see if they had cameras, which they don't. Cadaver's does, but I don't have the hacking skills required to check the footage from Monday night." I looked at Amy. "Am I forgetting anything?"

"The key."

Right. "She also found Jessica's assistant's keys in her car, and she thinks someone planted it there to frame her. She also drank a bottle of essential oil, thinking it was vodka, which is why she's so green."

"Anything else?" Chase asked.

"I think that's a fair synopsis of the situation."

Chase nodded to Hampton. Hampton nodded back and walked into Cadaver's Caverns.

"You two are something else." Chase ran a hand down his face. "Where are the keys?'

"I have them." Amy pulled the keys from her pocket.

Chase heaved a sigh. Not a sigh of relief. More of a frustrated, why-didn't-you-call-the-police-when-you-found-the-keys, thanks-for-putting-your-fingerprints-all-over-it, I-literally-can't-do-anything-with-this-now, type of sigh. He pulled on a pair of gloves, took the keys from her, and read the tag.

"That's her address alright," Chase said. "We've been looking for these."

"I think it should be noted that any smart killer wouldn't have left incriminating evidence on their backseat for all to see," I said. "It obviously was a plant."

"Not all murderers are smart," he said.

"Good point."

Hampton returned and nodded to Chase. Chase nodded back.

"There's no footage of you walking outside Cadaver's on Monday night," Chase said to Amy.

"How do you know?" I asked. "Did you talk to the owner, Chuck?"

"Hampton was able to access the security cameras. *He* has hacking abilities. "

"I called the owner," Hampton said.

"There was no footage of the front door? Was it erased?" I asked. "How can you have an entire warehouse of expensive movie props and no cameras angled at the front door to see who comes in and out?"

Chase shook his head. "No. The camera wasn't positioned in a way that provided a clear picture of the outside."

"You got all that from a nod?" I asked.

"Yes." Chase held the keys out to Hampton.

Hampton slipped on a pair of gloves, took the keys, and went to the trunk to put them in a bag.

"When was the last time you drove your car?" Chase asked Amy.

"Yesterday, when I came home from the studio. Around 5 PM."

"Are you sure it wasn't in there yesterday?" he asked.

Amy hugged her middle. "I'm sure…I think…I don't know."

Helpful.

"When you filmed with Jessica on Monday, did she appear upset?" Chase asked.

Amy snorted. "Upset? Try a royal—"

"Bleep!" I said and jerked my head toward Lilly, who was still at the helm of my car "driving."

Amy closed her eyes as if a curse-word alternative were written on the back of her lids. "Fine. She was being a witch. More so than usual. At one point Lance pulled her aside and tried to comfort her. She was mad about a fundraiser the two did together over the weekend. I'm not sure what happened, but I overheard them talking about it. Something about security guards and relatives? You should talk to Lance."

"You haven't heard?" Hampton said.

"Heard what?" I asked.

Chase heaved another sigh. It was a bad-news-was-soon-to-follow type of sigh.

Hampton might be able to read Chase's nods. But I knew his sighs.

"This afternoon Lance Holstrom was found dead in his home," Chase said.

I gasped.

"Multiple gunshot wounds."

I gasped.

"It wasn't pretty."

Lance Holstrom played Frank Darling, Lola Darling's current *and* ex-husband—it was gripping television. He had lush blond hair, artificially bronzed skin, and pouty lips—what he was known for. I'd never met Lance. Amy had said he was a multitalented and gracious actor, and now *he* was dead.

What a lousy week for Hollywood.

Amy freaked. "Can someone please tell me what the hell is happening? Is there a crazy murderer on the loose, killing off the entire cast?"

Neither Chase nor Hampton answered.

Comforting.

Amy bit her nail beds. "So someone broke into Lance's home and began shooting?"

"The killer didn't break in," said Hampton. "He opened fire from outside."

That was worse. I pictured Lance sitting on his couch, watching television when bullets blasted through the window and...*ugh*...having a vivid imagination is both a curse and a blessing.

Mostly a curse.

Lilly honked the horn and waved. We all waved back, and she went back to driving.

"We've put the entire cast on high alert," Chase said. "We're working with the network to up security, and I've arranged for you to go to a hotel."

Amy rubbed her stomach. "Which one?"

"I think the network booked you at the Ritz downtown. We'll take you now and finish our interview there," Chase said.

"I suppose that's OK." Amy perked up a little. "Give me a minute. I need to call Spencer and"—she hiccupped into her fist—"*vomit*."

Hampton rolled his eyes. "Celebrities," he said under his breath.

Amy grabbed her phone from the passenger seat and hustled to the trash can under the lamppost.

I smacked Chase on the arm. "A freaking five-star hotel? Why didn't you say that when you came to my door? I just walked into a museum of body parts!"

"I knew you were lying to me, Cambria. I played along to see what you two would do. If you'd told me the truth, this would have been done an hour ago."

I opened my mouth—to say what, I wasn't sure. Chase made an excellent point, and I had no retort, so I crossed my arms.

Lilly laid on the horn.

Amy barfed.

Hampton picked at his back teeth.

Not exactly how I pictured spending my birthday.

Chase wrapped his hand around my arm and pulled me aside, further out of Lilly's earshot range. "There's a killer out there taking out his victims, execution style. Why would you get yourself involved?"

I yanked my arm free. "Because I thought my best friend was being framed, and she was."

"You need to stay out of it, Cambria." He grabbed my cheeks and forced me to look him in the eyes. "I mean it."

"But—"

"No *buts*." He cut me off. "Stay out of it. This has nothing to do with you."

*Nothing to do with me? He's got to be kidding me.* "Amy is my best friend," I reminded him.

"I don't care. But I will arrest you if I think you'll interfere."

"You just want to put me in cuffs."

He arched an eyebrow. "This is true."

"You're hot when you're all detective-y."

"You're hot when you're not inserting yourself into a murder investigation."

"Fine." I surrendered, and Chase released my face. "But do you think Amy is really a suspect? Or in any danger?"

Chase shoved his hands into the front pocket of his slacks, his signature stance. "Avoiding us didn't exactly help her.

But whoever killed Jessica and Lance knew what they were doing. We're not dealing with an amateur. But that is not for public knowledge."

I pretended to zip my lips.

"It's best she stays at a place where we can better keep an eye on her," Chase said. "And where she'll be away from you and Lilly. I do have a patrol going by your apartments every thirty minutes, so don't worry if you see a squad car there."

"I thought you said this has *nothing* to do with me?"

Chase put a hand on my shoulder. "It's for my peace of mind. I want you and Lilly safe. So please don't go looking for trouble."

"If you want your mind to be at peace, you could put *me* up at the Ritz. I'd be more than happy to make that sacrifice."

He smiled. "Not how it works."

Lilly honked the horn. "Mom! You almost done?"

I held up one finger to signal I'd be right there.

"I'll let you go." Chase's expression softened, and he gently touched my cheek with his fingertips. "I'll be in contact. And please—trust that we'll take care of it. I don't want anything happening to you."

"I'll be good." I crossed my heart. "I'm guessing I still won't be seeing you for a while?"

He nodded. "We'll celebrate your birthday when this is over. I promise."

"That's fine," I said, relieved I wouldn't have to explain why I couldn't hang out with him tonight anyway.

He gave me a quick kiss and went to help Amy into the car.

I hollered after him, "If you change your mind and feel the need to put *me* up at a hotel, I hear the Four Seasons is nice."

# CHAPTER ELEVEN

————

*See also: Crisis Coordinator*

Lilly and I were back home before six. I was exhausted. Lilly was not. She was doing an interpretive dance routine.

First a donut.

Then a Slurpee.

She might never sleep again.

I plopped my bag down on the kitchen counter with a sigh and checked my phone. Tom hadn't called me back. I was in no mood to go out tonight. Not with Tom. Not with anyone. All I wanted was ice cream, a shower, and sleep.

Tom would understand once he heard about my day. I called his cell again. He didn't answer again, and his voicemail box was full. It wasn't like him not to check his messages.

I sent him a text: delivered but not read.

Facebook message: no reply.

Twitter: nada.

Snapchat: nothing.

Complete radio silence.

Crap. There was a serial killer on the loose. This was no time to go off the grid. Not that I necessarily thought Tom was a target. Since he wasn't an actor on the show. He didn't even watch *Ghost Confidential*. He called it cheesy. But still! I grabbed a pint of rocky road from the freezer and stuck it to my face to relieve the pressure mounting behind my eyeballs.

"Can I have some?" Lilly hopped on one foot.

"I think you've hit your sugar quota for the day."

"What's quota mean?"

"It means you've reached your limit."

"What does limit mean?"

"How about dinner?"

"*Vâng.*" She tossed her empty Slurpee into the trash can, skipped to the living room, and spun in circles.

Definitely hit her sugar quota.

I opened the fridge and grabbed the fixings for a quesadilla, my go-to dinner when I'm either low on food or energy. Tonight was both. I checked the time. It was already 6:45 PM.

Tom was late. It wasn't like him to be late. And if he were, he'd let me know. Unless he got my message and I was off the hook? But I had asked him to call me. And it was unlike Tom not to at least text back that he had received the message.

That gnawing feeling returned to my stomach.

"Hey, Lilly?" I called from the kitchen. "Can you tell me what Daddy had planned for my birthday?" I grabbed a grater from the cabinet and shredded the cheese over the tortilla.

Lilly was still spinning. "He said I'm not allowed to tell you."

I sprinkled the cheese with salt, folded the tortilla in half, and placed it in the microwave. "I know, sweetie, and you're such a good promise-keeper." I set the timer for thirty seconds and pressed start. "But this one time I think it would be OK if you gave me a hint."

Lilly stopped spinning and used the chair to steady her world. "Daddy said I was going to spend the night with Mr. and Mrs. Nguyen and he had an evil sparkle present for you and lots of people to play with."

*Um…what?*

The sparkle sounded intriguing. Evil? Not so much. And it was rather presumptuous for him to make sleepover arrangements.

Again, my source was three years old.

But still. She was basically a genius.

"Help!" Lilly whined. "My stomach hurts 'cause I drank all the oil." She was on her back with her tongue out.

*Oh geez.*

"Are you pretending to be Aunt Amy?"

"Yes." She smiled. "But me am so super starving."

I had to laugh. She was never hungry. She was only ever *starving*. Then she'd take one bite and be "so super full."

I grabbed the quesadilla from the microwave, stepped over her, and set the plate on the table. "Your dinner is served, mademoiselle."

She looked up at me from the floor. "Daddy will feed me when me so super starving."

"It's *I*, and that doesn't surprise me." I tickled her stomach. She curled into a ball and giggled. "You want me to feed you like a baby, huh?" She giggled harder. "Huh?"

"Yes!" she yelled between breaths. "Feed me!"

My phone buzzed from the counter. I leapt over Lilly to answer. *Blocked Call* was printed across the top of the screen. "Hello?"

"Are you drowning in debt?" a cheerful woman asked. "Speedy Advances is your answer…"

*Click.*

"Was that the emergency line?" Lilly asked, still on the ground.

"No, it wasn't." I checked the time: 7:00 PM. "Go eat, please."

I called Tom's cell. It went straight to a full voicemail box again.

OK, so the worst-case scenario portion of my brain said: Something wasn't right.

The logical portion of my brain said: Something most definitely wasn't right.

The two rarely agreed.

I rubbed my neck…*hold on.* Emergency line! Tom's firm had a 24/7 emergency line.

Was it reserved for clients?

Yep.

Was I a client?

Nope.

But Tom was not answering his phone or texts, and it was now past seven. That classified as an emergency in my book.

I googled *Thomas Dryer Los Angeles attorney emergency line* and was directed to his bio on the firm's website.

*Thomas J. Dryer, Attorney at Law, is an experienced, dedicated*…yadda-yadda-yadda…scroll…scroll…scroll… *After he graduated from North Tahoe high school, he attended UCLA for both his undergrad and law school*…yadda-yadda-yadda. Skim…skim…skim. *You can reach Tom for after-hour emergencies at 888-JKL-LAWS.*

Bingo.

I drummed my fingers on the counter while the phone rang in my ear.

"JKL law offices. How can I help you?"

It was Margie, one of the partner's wives. She was married to the *K*. JKL was a small law firm based out of a closet-sized office in Downtown. JKL focused their efforts on low-income clientele, pro bono cases, and protecting the innocent. Aka: they were lucky to pay the electric bill. I'd met Margie at Lilly's second birthday party. She'd bought her a toy megaphone.

Margie was not invited to Lilly's third birthday party.

"Margie, it's Cambria Clyne. Sorry to call on the emergency line, but have you heard from Tom?" I yanked the lid off the ice cream and shoved a spoon in. "He's not answering his phone, and I'm worried."

"Let me ask Louie. I know he went to Tom's closing arguments today in Lancaster. Hold on."

Lancaster is on the outer edge of Los Angeles County. It could take anywhere from one to three hours to get there, depending on traffic.

Margie returned. "Cambria, Louie told me they finished in court around two and as far as he knew, Tom left right after him. They haven't talked since."

"He left around two?" I choked on my ice cream. "Are you sure?"

"According to Louie, Tom rushed out of there because it's your birthday today and he had a big surprise planned. Is everything OK?"

*Is everything OK?*

No!

Tom left five hours ago! I didn't care how bad traffic was—it wasn't five hours' worth, and even if it was, that left plenty of time to call and say he was running late.

I hung up with Margie.

Actually, I hung up *on* Margie. Tom was in trouble. There was no time for pleasantries. I had hospitals to call, traffic reports to comb through, and ulcers to form.

I rushed to my desk and turned on the computer. My hand bumped into *Mom*, and she crashed into the telephone, causing a small scratch along the bottom of the urn. I put her back and pulled up the LA County Traffic Alert website. Over 200 traffic collisions had been reported within the last five hours. I swear the requirements for obtaining a license within the Los Angeles County borders were at least two of the following:

One: text *only* when driving.

Two: become an inconsiderate prick.

Three: never use a turn signal.

Four: drive a BMW.

Eight of the accidents had happened between Los Angeles and Lancaster. Two reported a serious injury. Now it was time to call hospitals.

I started with the one closest to the first reported accident. When the operator answered, I explained who I was and why I was calling. Then I explained a second time because I was hard to understand when I was panicking.

"Ma'am," the operator said. "I'm sorry, but it's against hospital policy to give out patient information over the phone."

"So you're saying Thomas Dryer *is* a patient?"

"I didn't say that. What I said is, we're not allowed to give out any information over the phone."

"Fine!" I hit the End button on my cell really hard. It looked like I was going to Lancaster. "Lilly, honey." I attempted to keep my voice steady. "I have to take you back to Mr. and Mrs. Nguyen's house. You can finish your dinner there." I dumped her quesadilla into a Ziploc and returned the ice cream to the freezer.

Lilly melted into the chair. "But we *just* got home."

"I know, and you've been such a good champ, but this is important."

"I don't want to. I want to stay here!" She kicked the chair.

This was no time to argue with a three-year-old. I tossed a protesting Lilly onto my hip, grabbed my keys, swung the door open, and...

"Noooo!"

# CHAPTER TWELVE

———

*See also: Just a girl standing in front of a man asking him not to screw her over*

Tom stood there with his hair pointed heavenward, and his stress creviced deep between his brows. I slapped him across the face.

"Ouch!" He rubbed his cheek. "What'd you do that for?"

"I…I don't know…" I'd never slapped anyone before. But seeing Tom alive made me…*angry.* Angry at him for having put me through the torture of thinking he'd been hurt.

"I'm sorry." I touched the hand imprint on his cheek. "My nerves are all over the place. I thought you were killed or hurt…" My voice cracked.

"Shhhhh, it's OK. Come here." Tom wrapped his arms around us. Lilly was still on my hip, holding her bagged quesadilla, not impressed. I closed my eyes and soaked in Tom's warmth and relished in his touch and familiar scent—except— *yuck.* He smelled like day-old coffee.

"Didn't you get my email?" he asked.

"Email?" I looked at him. "What year is this? 1999? Why would you send an email instead of calling me?"

"Because someone stole my phone." Based on his expression, this was covered in the email. "I didn't remember your number off the top of my head. I sent the email to your gmail account."

Oh. I rarely checked my personal account. It had been overtaken by ads and messages of unclaimed lottery winnings.

"Daddy, where's your shoe?" Lilly giggled and pointed down to Tom's foot.

"It's out here drying because I stepped in a pile of dog poop on the lawn."

Lilly scrunched her nose. "*Ew*."

"Dog poop. On the lawn? In this courtyard?" I put Lilly down, went to the window above the couch, and pushed a blind slat out of the way. "Where was it?"

"Is it important?" Tom came inside and shut the door behind him.

"Yes. No cats or dogs allowed, and I have my inspection tomorrow." I pulled the blinds back further. A tiny light flickered. I cupped my hands against the window and squinted. It was Daniella from Apartment 13. She was on all fours, with her phone light on, crawling around on the grass.

Two thoughts.

The first: I didn't care to explore further.

The second: Daniella had snuck in a dog, it pooped on the lawn, and she was looking for it.

Either way: crap.

"Stay here. I have to go take care of this." I started for the door.

Tom grabbed my hand. "There's no time. We have to hurry."

Right. Going out. Obviously Tom didn't get my message. I wasn't in the mood to go anywhere but my bedroom—to sleep. And I was about to tell him just that, but he *had* gone through a great deal of trouble to get here. And a night out *could* take my mind off the serial killer attempting to frame Amy. And I *was* curious as to where we were going. And I *did* flat-iron Einstein.

"Fine," I said with a relenting sigh. "I'll talk to Daniella tomorrow."

"Good. I'll take Lilly to the Nguyens', and you can get ready. But be quick."

*Get ready?*

I was ready.

I'd been ready!

I checked my reflection in the window—Einstein was still in place. My makeup was smudged under the eyes, but not bad. I had the purple shirt and dark jeans on. I looked pretty darn good.

Perhaps jeans weren't the right attire?

I should probably check my email.

*Cam,*

*Bad news. My briefcase was stolen at the courthouse, and I'm at the police station right now filing a report. Traffic is terrible, and I won't be there until closer to 7. We'll need to leave right away. I have a big birthday surprise for you. Dress is semiformal. See you soon.*

*Happy Birthday!*

*XOXO Tom*

*Sent at 5:06 PM.*

XOXO?

Tom had never XO'd me before. Last year, he sent me a text saying *we need to talk*, with a heart emoji and a wink. I thought he was going to talk about *us*. I thought he'd tell me that he'd loved me all along, that I made him want to be a better man, that it'd always been me, that I had bewitched his body and soul, that I had him at "hello."

I might also watch too many romance movies.

At the very least, I thought he'd say he *liked* me.

I'd thought wrong.

It turned out all he wanted to talk about was the weather.

*Me (batting my baby blues): I got your text. What did you want to talk about?*

*Tom: It's been cold.*

*Me: Well, yeah, it is November.*

*Tom: We should get Lilly a nice jacket.*

*Me: That's probably a good idea.*

The man was a pansy when it came to commitment. There was no use reading too much into the *XO*. At least the email explained why he smelled like a police station.

I changed into a black shift dress and black suede lace-up sandals with two-inch heels. Yes, I looked ready for a funeral. Only because it was the exact outfit I wore to my Grandma Ruthie's funeral—when I was pregnant.

*Note to self: stop wearing maternity clothes.*

I threw a gold necklace on, removed the smudges from under my eyes, and I was good to go wherever it was we were going.

Tom was waiting for me in the living room, carving grooves into the carpet while he studied his watch.

"I'm ready." I held my arms out to the side and did a little spin. "Is this formal enough?"

Tom glanced up. "You look...*nice*."

"Don't sound so surprised."

"I'm not...it's just...you look gorgeous, Cam."

I felt myself blush. "Thanks."

"OK. We've got to hurry." He turned me around and put a blindfold over my eyes. "Can you see?"

I imagined him waving his hand in front of my face. "No, I can't." This was all rather exhilarating. I'd never been blindfolded before. Tom grabbed my hand and led me outside. "Wait. I have to set the alarm for my apartment."

"Is the office alarm set?" he asked.

"Yes."

"We'll lock the door. It will be fine for a few hours."

I heard the jiggle of my keys and the click of the deadbolt. We stopped so Tom could put his shoe on. Then he led me through the courtyard. My legs felt like Jell-O from the juxtaposition of shocks. I went from thinking Tom had been seriously injured, or even dead, to him dragging me around blindfolded for a birthday surprise.

I felt wisps of wind on my face and heard the parking lot gate open and close, footsteps, whisperings, the *click* of the locks on Tom's old green 4Runner.

"We're taking your car?" I asked.

"Yes. Let me help you in." He held me by the elbow and eased me in. I rammed my head into the roof. My knee into the door, and whacked my funny bone on the dash.

"Couldn't you have put the blindfold on me *after* I got in the car?"

Tom paused. "Probably. I had a whole thing planned, and now I'm improvising."

I blindly buckled my seat belt, and Tom pulled it tight. "You're going to like this, Cam." He brushed my cheek with his fingertips before he slammed the door shut.

Goose bumps erupted down my arms, and excitement fizzed in my stomach. No one had ever put together such a grand gesture for me.

The driver's side door opened. The engine revved, and we were moving. I pictured Tom's hands, white-knuckled at ten and two on the steering wheel. I could picture the inside of the car. The breath mints in the cup holder, along with the loose change, ChapStick, and a jail visitor sticker. The tan upholstery would be free from trash, dashboard clean, with a box of Clorox wipes tucked under my seat. Lilly's booster in the back with a bottle of water in the cup holder. A mesh bag of toys hung around the back of Tom's headrest.

We took a hard right, and I held on to the grab handle. Based on the sound and speed of the car, I presumed we were on the freeway.

I readjusted in my seat, resolute to enjoy the spoils. So what if my eyeballs were digging into my brain and the seat belt was digging into my shoulder? Grandma Ruthie used to say, "Enjoy the ride, no matter how bumpy it is."

"I'm sorry about your phone and briefcase," I said once we were on the way.

"Me too." Tom paused.

I heard the *blink-bloop* of the blinker, and we veered to the left.

"Do you have any idea who could have taken it or when?" I asked.

Tom pumped the breaks. My head fell forward. He slammed on the gas. My head fell back. "I have no idea who took it," he said. "I left my briefcase on the bench while I consulted with a client. Luckily, my keys and wallet were in my pocket. But without my phone, I'm screwed. The only password I could remember off the top of my head was my email."

We veered to the right. To the left. To the right. Gas. Brake. Gas. Veer. Brake.

The fizz of excitement was gone. My stomach was not impressed with Tom's driving. I felt around the center console for the mints I was sure were there. My Grandma Ruthie used to say, "There's no ailment a mint can't cure." I grabbed the roll of Certs and popped two into my mouth.

*Blech.*

Grandma Ruthie had never driven with Tom.

"So how was your day?" Tom asked, attempting to sound breezy, but I could hear the stress in his voice.

I told him about our trip to Cadaver's Caverns, Amy being framed, and Lance Holstrom, which he'd yet to hear about.

"I swear this sounds exactly like an episode of *Ghost Confidential*," he said.

"Since when did you start watching *Ghost Confidential*? I thought it was *cheesy*?" The Tom I knew watched sports, action movies, and television shows where people talked about sports.

"It is. I don't watch that crap. I'm just guessing." Tom reached for my hand and intertwined his fingers with mine. Tom and I didn't *do* handholding either. This was all rather confusing, slash exciting, slash nauseating.

"I'm glad Amy is in a hotel," Tom said. "She needs to keep her distance from you and Lilly. You don't want to get mixed up with a hit man."

"How do you know it's a hit man?"

"From everything I've read, and from what you just told me, it sounds like the work of a contracted killer. A hit man gets the job done and gets out. It's bam-bam-bam-bam hit all vital organs, you're dead."

*Blech.* "That's a lovely visual."

"It's not a pretty subject. I've spent the last six weeks researching it."

"How'd it go today?"

"Jury is still out."

*Blink-bloop*

*Swerve.*

*Brake.*

*Gas.*

*Blech.*

*Enjoy the ride, Cambria. Enjoy the ride.*

"Are you OK?" Tom asked.

"Mmmmhmmm." I stifled a burp and cleared my throat. "I have a question for you. Why did you tell our daughter you were taking me out and that you had a big surprise for me?"

"Because I knew she'd tell you."

*Wait...what?* "Why did you want her to ruin it?"

"I didn't want her to ruin it. I...it doesn't matter."

*Blink-bloop.*

*Swerve.*

*Brake.*

*Belch.*

"It matters to me," I said.

"I didn't want to chicken out," he said, barely above a whisper. "I was going to ask you last night, but *he* was there. What's with you two anyway? Are you really that into him?"

"Yes," I said without having to think. I was into Chase. Very much so.

I wished I could see Tom's expression.

"He seems like a pansy," he said. "I don't like him."

"Chase is a detective for the LAPD. I hardly think that qualifies him as a pansy."

*Swerve.*

*Brake.*

*Gas.*

*Blech.*

*Clank.*

The clank was new and followed by a *clunk* and a *thud.* Not that I was a mechanic, but even my car didn't make those noises. Nor did it have the metal-on-metal scent.

Suddenly a centrifugal force pushed the back of my head against the seat. We spun until we flipped. I held tight to the seat belt. We went upside down, right side up, upside down, right side up until we flipped one last time to an upright position.

Pretty sure this wasn't part of the surprise.

# CHAPTER THIRTEEN

———

*See also: Ouch*

I appeared to be in a parallel universe where hearts raced, bodies moved slowly, lights flashed, police waved traffic along, and no one made sense.

*Why am I on the side of the freeway?*

*Why is there so much traffic?*

*Why are there flares on the road?*

*Why is Tom in my face talking to me?*

"Cansh lue blandesh aaap," Tom said and stared at me as if I too were fluent in gibberish.

"Huh?" I asked.

"Can you stand up?" he repeated in English.

*I don't know. Can I?*

I went to my knees first, then to my feet.

*I guess I can.*

I clutched on to Tom's arm for support when it hit me like a fast pitch to the face. We were in a car accident!

A bad car accident! After we'd tumbled, and tumbled, and tumbled, the car came to an absolute stop. Silence. An eerie stillness that seemed to stretch on for hours but, in reality, was seconds. The roof had been an inch from my head. Smoke had hissed from the front hood. The airbags had deployed, and I had smelled the suffocating stench of gunpowder.

Tom and I had shared a look. A small stream of blood had dribbled down the side of his cheek. The shock on his face had mirrored my own. In one swift motion, he'd unbuckled his seat belt and reached for me. He'd been talking—saying what?

I'd had no idea. There'd been unfamiliar faces. Sirens. Then, somehow, I'd ended up outside.

Holy crap.

An ambulance was parked behind the pile of metal that was once Tom's 4Runner. Traffic was at a standstill. Tom's little SUV had landed on an embankment near a chain-link fence and a homeless man's tent, but everyone had to stop and stare.

Two minivans and a Porsche were pulled along the side of the freeway with their emergency lights on. All three vehicles were unscathed. The blue van belonged to a labor and delivery nurse who was on her way home when she'd seen us rolling across the freeway. I listened to her recount the event to the police officer.

"It happened so fast. All of a sudden the car swerved and then rolled. It's a miracle they didn't hit anyone else."

The woman from the Porsche, and the man from the other minivan, gave the same account: *all of a sudden...swerved...rolled...miracle.*

Tom, too, was speaking to a cop, a CHP with a handlebar mustache. "My check engine light flashed. Then I lost control." He wrapped his hand around his neck and winced.

"Do you recall how fast you were going?" the CHP asked Tom.

"No more than sixty-five," he said.

The CHP's eyes cut to me. "Do you remember?"

"I was blindfolded. I don't know how fast we were going," I answered.

The officer blinked. "You were blindfolded?"

"It's her birthday, and I was surprising her," Tom quickly added. "We were on our way to see *Wicked*." He pointed to the billboard ten yards ahead of us advertising *Wicked now playing at the Pantages Theater.*

My heart skipped a beat. *Wicked!*

Seeing *Wicked* had been a dream of mine for years. Lilly and I listened to the soundtrack, and I knew every word. Tickets were over a hundred dollars for nosebleed seats. I couldn't justify the expense. But Tom could. He could justify the cost for me. And he didn't part with money easily. I was touched.

This explained the "evil" and the "people to play with."

The sparkle? Not so much.

Tom's broken front window did sparkle under the freeway lights. Unless our daughter had psychic abilities, I guessed the sparkle came after the evil.

# CHAPTER FOURTEEN

———

*See also: Conspiracy Theorist*

I sat, squished between the tow truck driver and Tom. The cabin smelled like mustard. My legs were ankle-deep in McDonald's Big Mac wrappers. The tow truck driver's name was Rick. He was a nice fellow—had a goatee that nearly touched his navel and holes the size of quarters in each ear.

Tom and I sat, stiff as a board. Being in a car again was unnerving.

"Looked like your pistons blew right through your cylinder." Rick had one hand on the steering wheel and the other holding a 32-ounce McDonald's cup. I'd have felt a lot better if he'd had both hands on the wheel. "When was the last time you changed your oil, man?"

"Last week," Tom said without taking his eyes off the road.

Rick snorted. "Then you must've been leakin', or someone hates ya. The steering pump busted too. You're lucky to be sittin' here. Shoot."

Rick pulled over in front of the apartment building. The streets were lined with cars parked for the night. "Thanks for the ride home," Tom said and extended a hand to help me out of the cab.

"Not a problem, man," Rick said. "You guys get some rest. You got the information for the junkyard. Just give us a call after you talk to your insurance."

Tom swung the door shut, and we waved goodbye to Rick as he drove away with what was left of Tom's car strapped to the bed. What a sad piece of green metal. It was hard to believe we were standing there without injury. The paramedic had advised us to go to the hospital. We declined. An emergency room bill would hurt more than any pain I was currently experiencing.

We managed to transfer Lilly from the Nguyen's apartment to her bed without waking her. Once she was safely relocated and tucked in, Tom walked to the living room and flopped onto the couch. His long body took up the entire length, leaving his feet hanging off the side. "I imagined this day going a lot differently," he muffled into the fake leather cushion.

I sat on the floor beside him, crisscrossed my legs, and leaned back on the palms of my hands. "It's the thought that counts?"

Tom reached out and cupped my face. "I'll see if I can get us tickets next week."

I leaned into his touch. "Don't worry about it. Save your money. We'll catch it next year."

Tom dropped his hand with a loud thump. "I'm going to have to get a new phone and a new car." He flipped to his back and draped his arm over his eyes. "I thought I had another solid hundred thousand miles left on that car."

"Did your landlord say anything about you leaking oil in your carport?" I asked.

Tom shook his head.

"Did the car give you any trouble this morning?"

He shook his head.

"Was your oil light on?"

He shook his head.

I brought my elbows to my knees. "Rick said your piston went through your cylinder. Is that why we flipped?" I wasn't proficient in car.

"When there's not enough oil, the metals rub up against each other and the engine seizes. Which is why the pistons blew through the cylinder. I felt the car sputter, but I didn't lose control until I went to pull over and the wheel locked. Debris must have got stuck in the power steering pump. Just a bad coincidence, that's all."

Coincidence? Grandma Ruthie used to say, "Coincidence is an explanation used by fools and liars."

I thought of an episode of *If Only*, where Bobbie Dart's husband's new girlfriend had drained the oil in Bobbie's vehicle. Bobbie had crashed and had been in a coma for three weeks before she regained consciousness. Yikes.

"What if someone did this so *we* would get into a car accident?" I said, thinking out loud. "You got your oil changed last week. And I know your landlord would tell you if you were leaking in the carport. And what are the odds that your steering pump valve thing would get jammed? Rick said either you were leaking oil or someone hates you. I'm sure someone hates you."

Tom peered at me from under his arm. "Like who?"

"Someone you went up against in court?"

"I doubt it. No DA is going to go through the hassle of draining my oil on the chance I'd get into a wreck," he said.

"A client you lost the case for?"

"If I lost the case, they'd be in jail. Also, I don't lose."

I bit at my lip until another idea trotted into my head. "Then it's probably one of the many women you've slept with and didn't call back. Let me get a paper. We'll make a list of the names you can remember and start from there."

"Don't bother. It's been months."

"Months?" I repeated to be sure I heard him right. Tom had at least one new fling a week.

"Yes, *months*."

"Dry spell?"

"Something like that."

"That's a bummer."

"You're telling me."

"No sex *and* no oil."

"And no phone, and no car, and no briefcase," he said.

Typically I could count on Tom to be the Pollyanna in any situation. Poor guy looked defeated, lying there on my couch. He needs sugar, I thought. I grabbed what was left of the rocky road from the freezer and retrieved the bag of Halloween candy hidden in the cabinet. Pretty sure that stuff never expires.

I padded back to my spot on the floor and handed Tom a spoon. "Dig in. This will help."

Tom sat up and patted the spot beside him on the couch. I slid beside him and tucked my legs under my butt. He took a scoopful of ice cream, and I started with a bite-sized Butterfinger.

"Feel better?" I asked.

"No."

"Keep eating. It takes a while for the calories to kick in." I unwrapped a Milky Way. "Maybe Amy was right and this is all the urn's fault."

Tom gave me a sideways glance. "Care to explain?"

"Apartment 17 moved out, and I found an urn in her carport cabinet yesterday morning and put it on my desk."

"Why would you put it on your desk?"

"It felt disrespectful to put her in the storage closet. There are spiders in there. "

"*Her*?"

"Mom. And Amy said harboring an urn that doesn't belong to you disturbs the deceased and causes bad luck. Not that I believe in all that. It's getting harder to discredit her theory. But what I don't understand is why I would get cursed. It's not like I'm the one who forgot her."

"You hang around Amy too much."

"Trust me. I thought she was full of crap when she told me, but since I've had the urn, the lobby burned down, Jessica Wilders was killed, Lance Holstrom was killed, someone tried to frame Amy, there was a giant spider in here this morning, we got into a car accident, your phone was stolen..." I nearly inhaled the Pixie Stick I was working on.

"What's wrong now?"

I turned to face Tom. "Do you think whoever killed Jessica and Lance is the one who messed with your car?"

This got a laugh out of Tom.

"I'm serious," I said. "There's a killer on the loose, and we were just in a horrible car accident. We could have died."

"If someone really wanted us dead, there are better ways than draining my oil."

"What if they wanted it to look like an accident," I said. "They were mad that I was snooping around, trying to exonerate Amy."

"The murderer is using a gun and targeting celebrities. I'm a lawyer. You're an apartment manager. There's no connection."

"Amy," I reminded him.

Tom smacked his forehead. "You kill me."

"No, but someone else might."

He reached into the Halloween bag and grabbed a Three Musketeer bar. "You're attempting to make something out of nothing."

I nearly choked on my Reese's. "Out of nothing? We almost died. How is that nothing? Did you hit your head?"

"Don't take this the wrong way, Cam. But you tend to plug farfetched theories into innocuous circumstances to turn them into *Law & Order*–worthy criminal cases."

"How can I not take that personally?" I said. "And also, no I don't."

"All those crime shows you watch skew your perception of reality."

"I don't watch *that* many."

As exhibit A, Tom turned on the television and clicked to my DVR. "We have *Mickey Mouse Clubhouse, Law & Order SVU, Criminal Minds, Chicago PD, New York PD, Dallas PD, Seattle PD, Miami PD, If Only*, and...*WWE Monday Night Raw*?"

I yanked the remote away from him. "I got sucked in to a fight the other night."

Tom ran a hand down his face. "All I'm saying is, you don't have anything to worry about. My car was old, it broke, and we had an accident. This has nothing to do with an urn or Lola and Frank Darling."

"Lola and Frank Darling?" I rose to my knees and pointed at him. "You *do* watch *Ghost Confidential*!"

"I may have caught an episode here and there."

"Liar. You watch it, and you like it."

"Fine." He put his palms up. "I watch it, and I like it. Gives me something to do at night."

"Dry spell?"

"Yep."

"Welcome to my life."

We cheered our spoons.

"By the way, I'm spending the night," he said.

"What?" Ice cream dribbled down my chin.

"I don't have a car."

"You can Uber."

"I don't have my phone."

"You can Uber."

"It's best I stay here."

"You can Uber."

"I'll sleep on the couch. Come here." Tom shoved Einstein to the side and massaged my shoulders. At first, I resisted. But slowly, the tightness melted as his thumbs worked out the knots, and eventually I went limp. "Feel good?"

"Mmmmhmmmm. But I'm not breaking your dry spell."

*Note to self: try really, really hard not to break Tom's dry spell.*

# CHAPTER FIFTEEN

———

*See also: Oops*

I woke the next morning to the wind whistling through the cracks in the windowsill and the sunlight warm against my eyelids. I buried my throbbing head into the pillow, trying for another few minutes of sleep, but couldn't get there. Then came my upstairs neighbor Mickey—*swoosh, slam, psshhhh, thud!*

Moaning, I flipped my sore body to the side, careful not to wake Tom. He was sprawled out like he fell asleep mid-snow angel. I couldn't let him sleep on the uncomfortable couch, not after we'd just been in a car accident. He deserved the marshmallow bed. Tom still had on his day-old coffee clothing (I guess it would be two days now). I was in my maternity funeral dress. We were both too exhausted for personal hygiene, which decreased the temptation by 50 percent.

I'd fallen into a fitful slumber within minutes of landing on my bed and had dreamt of zombies, urns, severed feet, and Jessica Wilders. This time she beat me on the back of the head with a piston. Lance Holstrom, Chase, Rick the tow truck driver, and Tom were all watching from the sidelines, wearing McDonald's uniforms.

I should have skipped the Halloween candy.

Tom's arm curled around me and pulled me closer. His body was warm, familiar, strong, and safe. I thought about how good he felt next to me. Then I thought about how wrong that thought was. Then I tried to recall why it was so wrong. Then I remembered Chase. But then I couldn't remember if we'd ever agreed not to sleep with other fully clothed people. Then I remembered the years I'd spent pining over Tom only to be sent to Alcatraz. Then I thought about the multiple lifeboats he'd thrown me over the last six months and how I still was neither on the mainland nor on Alcatraz, but floating somewhere in-between, seasick, sunburned, dehydrated, and tired. Then I thought about the number of times he'd been there for me when I needed legal help. I thought about what an amazing father he was. The tears in his eyes when he held our little girl for the first time. The look on his face when she took her first steps. He loved her, and deep down, I think he loved me too. And that scared him. That scared the hell out of him. With me, there was no casual dating. It was all or nothing.

Then I thought about the number of times I'd gotten my hopes up only to be crushed. I thought about the hundreds of women who had woken up beside him, and that thought made me mad.

I slowly flipped to my stomach and looked at Tom. It was hard to be mad at that cute mug. He really was handsome. His nose was the perfect shape for his face. Not too big or too small, it had a sloping tip that blended perfectly down. His lips were full. The light freckles dotting his nose. The single worry line creviced between his brows. The giant spider crawling across his face—

The giant spider crawling across his face!

*It's back!*

"Tom," I panted. "Tom. Tom. Tom. Tom. Tom. Tom. Tom. Tom."

He squinted one eye open. "What?"

"Don't panic. But there's a massive spider on your face. Don't. Move."

Tom soared out of bed so fast you'd think he had wings. He smacked his head on the ceiling fan and danced around the room while I searched under the sheets.

"Where did it go?" he yelled.

"I don't know. Your dancing scared it off."

We hunted through the covers and tossed the comforter to the other side of the room, then the sheets, then the pillowcases, then the pillows, then the fitted sheet, then the pad, and then the mattress.

"It looked like a tarantula," Tom said from the floor, looking under my bed.

"It was here yesterday, and I put him outside." I moved the nightstand.

Tom pulled the bed frame away from the wall. "Why didn't you kill it?"

"I was trying to be nice!"

"Daddy?"

Tom and I froze. Me with the picture of the Los Angeles landscape over my head, Tom with the box spring hoisted up.

Lilly stood in the doorway with a seriously confused face on. "Why are you here, Daddy?"

Tom lowered the box spring. "I came to...to..."

We shared a look.

"Kill the spider," I said.

Lilly's eyes went wide. "Did you catch it?"

"*Erm*, no." I involuntarily shivered.

Her eyes went from Tom to me, and back again, with a mistrustful scrunch of her forehead. "Did you come 'cause you her boyfriend?" she said to Tom.

"No," Tom and I said in unison.

"Not at all," Tom added for emphasis, and I rolled my eyes. "Why don't you go play, and then we'll have breakfast together."

"You'll eat breakfast with us?" Lilly slapped her hands to her cheeks. "Best day ever!" She skipped to her room, not before stealing another look back with the biggest smile I'd ever seen.

Tom and I simultaneously exhaled and winced in pain. I felt like one big bruise with legs. My room was a mess. I heard my phone buzzing from...somewhere. We rummaged around until I found it under a blanket with a cracked screen.

Great.

I had two missed calls from Amy, nothing from Chase, and one alert: *Trustee meeting today.*

*Today?*

Today.

Today!

I freaked. "I have a meeting with Patrick and the trustee in a few hours!"

Tom put the mattress back. "Can you reschedule? Say you were in a car accident yesterday and need a day to recover?"

"Are you crazy?" I ran to my closet. The purple shirt was mangled on the floor. A quick sniff of the pits told me it was OK to wear again. I slid on a grungy sports bra (hello, uniboob). I had no other clean options. "Patrick would kill me, only after he fired me, if I canceled it." I buttoned up the shirt and *slowly* danced into a pair of black pants. "His only request was that today runs smoothly with no surprises. The trustee is over most of the properties Patrick manages, and this is the McMills' favorite place." I went to the bathroom and applied deodorant— six swipes. "I've worked too hard to get ready for this visit to let anything get in my way. This is my shot!"

"But aren't you sore?"

"My sternum hurts. Other than that, I'm fine." And by *hurt*, I meant it felt like it had snapped in half. But who needed a sternum?

Tom stood in the doorway and watched me brush my teeth. "I think you should tell Patrick that you need the day off."

"I can't." Actually, I probably could, given the circumstances, but I was determined to get my golf cart. A golf cart meant more money. More money meant more security for my kid. More security meant less therapy for her later in life—I hoped. "This meeting is too important for my career." I spat into the sink and wiped my mouth with a towel.

*Ouch.* Muscles I didn't even know existed hurt.

"So be it," Tom said with a shake of his head. "I can move a few things around and take Lilly if that will help."

My shoulders dropped in sweet relief. "That would be amazing."

*Amazing!*

Tom leaned against the doorframe, with his arms crossed, and took me in. "I had fun last night."

"Even if your dry spell continues?"

"I feel it coming to an end." He released his flirty side smirk. I knew that side smirk. It was the same one he gave me four years ago.

*Tom (with side smirk): What's your name?*
*Me: Cambria, what's yours?*

*Tom: Tom. Can I buy you a drink?*
*Me: I guess. But I'm not going home with you.*
*Fast-forward nine months: Hello, Lilly.*
Oh geez.

Tom went to make breakfast, and I called Amy. She answered on the third ring.

"How are you doing?" I asked.

"I'm freaking out! *Put it over there, thanks,*" she said to someone in the background. "Cambria, Zahra is dead!"

I gasped because that was my go-to, someone-famous-has-been-murdered reaction. Except, "Who is Zahra again?"

"She's Jessica's assistant! She was found early this morning at her home. Killed the same way. Multiple gunshot wounds."

Oh crap. No wonder I hadn't heard from Chase. This was getting serious. "Are you OK?"

"No! I've never been more stressed in all my life. Holed up here while people are dying. *I'll do the cucumber peel,*" she said.

"How much longer are you there?"

"I have no idea. *The egg white omelet, hold the spinach, add tomato.* Someone is clearly upset with Jessica and taking it out on everyone in her life. And they tried to peg the whole thing on me."

I'd be freaking out too. "Did they find any more information about the key or the phone call?"

"I don't know about the phone call. But they brought my car for CSI to examine and found a gun in my trunk, Cambria. A gun! *Please make sure the towels are steamed to 103 degrees.* I've never owned a gun. I've never fired a gun. Chase said they're running prints, or dusting for prints…something with prints."

I rubbed my sternum.

"Also this Dirty Dan blogger is at it again! *Please be sure the food doesn't touch.* He's saying that the detectives were at my door yesterday. Spencer thinks I should talk to Tom for legal advice in case this turns against me," Amy said. "But the turd isn't answering his phone."

"That's because his phone was stolen. He's here. I'll have him call you on my cell."

"Hold on. Tom is there at seven o'clock in the morning?" Amy's voice perked. "Tell me *everything*."

"It's not what you think. Nothing *happened*, happened. He was going to take me to see *Wicked*, but we got into a car accident before we got there. His car is totaled, so he stayed here, and his cell was stolen yesterday at the courthouse."

"His phone was stolen, and you two were in a car accident?" she drew out the words.

"Yes. Why? Do you know something?"

"Yes. It's all the urn's fault. *Is there kale in this?* I told you, Cambria. *The eggs and cheese can't touch.* The deceased has been disturbed, and now you're cursed. Your life will continue to be a series of unfortunate events until you die."

There was a lovely thought.

"I'm not cursed," I said. "I don't believe in all that. But let's just pretend I did. How might I un-disturb the dead?"

"Ask her what she wants. You'll also want salt and a black tourmaline crystal. It creates an electrical force field around your aura. Unless the spirit was sent to you intentionally. Then the black tourmaline won't work. Let me do some research on what crystal you should use."

Yeah, OK. She lost me.

"Are you listening to me, Cambria?"

"No."

"You…*pssshhhhh*…and…*pssssssshhhh*…trust me. *Spencer, honey, can you make sure they didn't put pepper on my omelet?*"

I plugged one ear. "Amy? You're breaking up."

"This is…you'll need a recorder…spirits speak at an octave we can't…*You can set up the massage table over there*…I better—"

My phone turned off. "What the heck?" I held down the Power button until the Apple logo flashed on the shattered screen. Even though I had ninety percent battery left, the phone turned off again.

So now I could add *buy new phone* to my to-do list. Great. At least Amy was safe and well pampered.

I finished applying my makeup and put Einstein in a low bun. I spritzed myself with perfume and took a step back, bumped into Tom, and let out a yelp.

"Tom, you scared me." I clutched my chest. "You can't be sneaking up on me like that. Not when there's a crazy killer out there and everyone is dying."

"Who died now?" Tom asked.

"Zahra, Jessica Wilders' assistant."

"The one who found Jessica dead?"

"The very one. She was at home. Multiple gunshot wounds." I grimaced. The whole thing was too horrible to comprehend.

Tom put a hand on my shoulder. "I know it's hard, but try not to stress. I'm sure they'll catch the guy soon."

"Or girl."

He rolled his eyes. "Fine. Girls can be murderers too."

"Darn right. But this isn't an equal rights thing. A woman called Amy pretending to be EJ Ryder's assistant. They should be looking for a woman. Also, Amy wants to speak to you. She needs legal advice. They took her car in and found a gun in the trunk."

"Is it her gun?"

"Amy has never owned a gun. They give her the heebie-jeebies."

"Is that a technical term?"

"It is now...wait, what are you hiding?" Tom's left arm was curled behind his back, and his side smirk had morphed into a mischievous grin.

I tried to see what he had, but he turned around. Could it be the sparkle? Lilly had been right about the evil play. Why not the rest?

"Let me see," I demanded.

Tom shook his head.

"Thomas James Dryer, let me see what you have behind your back."

"Close your eyes," he said.

"Fine." I did as instructed. "But last time you had me close my eyes, we almost died."

"We're not moving," he said in a low husky voice, and my insides clenched. "Now, hold out your hand."

I held out my hand and waited. Tom placed a light cardboard box into my waiting palm, and my breath hitched in my chest. What could the sparkle be? A necklace? Earrings? I didn't like wearing jewelry, but I'd made an exception for him.

"Now, open," Tom said.

Feeling excited, I opened my lids and looked down at the box in my hand. "Are you kidding me?" I threw the box of Thin Mints at him. "Freaking Tom. Why were you in my nightstand?"

Tom laughed and picked the cookies up off the ground. "I was looking to see if you had protection and found this instead."

With a grunt, I snatched the box from him. "You drive me crazy. I'm not ending your dry spell. Get out of my bathroom. And there better not be a single cookie missing," I said and winced. The stress of all these murders and Tom's flip-flopping around wasn't helping my post-crash pain.

"It was a joke." Tom turned me around and dug his fingertips into my neck.

It felt good last night. Then it felt like he was stabbing me with shards of glass.

"I'm sorry. I was just trying to lighten the mood. You don't have to stress about this right now," he said. "I'll take Lilly. You'll get through the meeting. It will all be alright." *Yeah, yeah, yeah.* Tom wasn't a worrier. It wasn't in his DNA.

For the record—it was in mine.

Tom worked his way down my arms. That felt good. "I do need to borrow your car so I can get a new phone," he said.

"My car?" I spun around and came face-to-face with his chest. "I would feel better if you used an Uber." Tom began to protest, and I cut him off. "What if someone *did* something to my car? I would be on edge all day thinking of you and Lilly driving around."

"No one did anything to my car, Cam. It was an accident."

"Accident or not, I won't be able to concentrate if you take my car," I said, unyielding.

"Fine, but only because you said *please*."

"I didn't say *please*."

"You should."

The man drove me crazy. "*Please*?"

"OK." Tom leaned down and kissed me. I stiffened. *What is happening?* Tom and I didn't *do* kissing. But his lips were warm against mine, and I allowed myself to enjoy the contact. He then kissed me again. And again. And again. Each time harder and more fervent. His mouth tasted like mint and chocolate. His hands traveled down my back. I found myself pulling him closer. Our tongues met. My hands were on his face, in his hair, on his chest.

Tom hoisted me up onto the counter. I wrapped my legs around him. His mouth traveled down my neck, and I panted.

"Can someone turn on the TV?" Lilly yelled from the living room.

*No!*

Tom and I parted. Our chests pumped and faces flushed, desire swirled. He placed his forehead against mine, and I closed my eyes.

"It's not working!" Lilly yelled. "Never mind. It turned on"

Tom cupped my cheek in the palm of his hand and looked me square in the eyes. Hazel on blue. My heart hammered in my chest. I thought he was going to kiss me again, and I licked my lips, waiting. Tom gulped and traced his finger along my jawline. I closed my eyes, ready…and…and…*aaannnnddddd*…nothing. Absolutely nothing.

Tom turned around and left, closing the door behind him.

What. The. Hell?

I let out a grunt and winced. It wasn't going to be a good day. I could feel it. I could feel it deep in my sore twenty-nine-year-old sexually frustrated bones.

# CHAPTER SIXTEEN

———

*See also: Garbage Man*

And I was right.

"Strong winds expected to blast Southern California today," the local newscaster announced during the Early Morning Show. "Winds or gusts of 35 mph are anticipated, making travel difficult and causing possible widespread power outages. High wind advisory in effect until 5:00 PM!" He flashed a megawatt smile and performed his signature fist pump.

*This is why I don't watch the news.*

I slid open the blinds and gazed out the window. All I saw was trash. So. Much. Trash. Fast-food containers, flyers, receipts, debris, soda cans. Trash scattered across the grass. Trash in the walkways. Trash in the pool. Trash stuck in the trees. The trash can itself had blown over. A tumbleweed rolled by.

A tumbleweed!

We lived in the middle of the city. Where did a tumbleweed come from? *Dorothy and Toto should be here any minute*, I thought.

My original plan for the day—let's call it Plan A—consisted of Lilly and me going for a stroll through the property, to be sure all was in order. Which of course it would be because this was Plan A. I'd skim over reports and wipe down my desk. After, we'd go to Noah's Bakery down the street and purchase half-a-dozen fresh-from-the-oven bagels, along with three different types of cream cheese (strawberry, regular, and chive) because options were important. We'd then swing by Trader Joe's for a spring arrangement of roses and Peruvian lilies. Come eleven I'd have the bagels stacked on a glass platter in the middle of my kitchen table (because we no longer had a lobby), along with the variety of cheeses and small bottles of water with Elder Property Management labels on them, 'cause in Plan A I was crafty. The flowers would be in a glass vase next to the brochures. I'd be sitting at my desk, with my ankles crossed, wardrobe pristine, smile in place, like a wild-haired June Cleaver, very much the perfect hostess.

Plan A blew away.

Moving on.

Plan B: Run like a mad woman through the property to be sure there were no obvious infractions. Pick up as much trash as possible. Deliver Three-Day Notices to those who had yet to pay rent.

Should that go south, there was always Plan C: Fake my death to get out of the meeting.

At least I had options.

Tom actively avoided eye contact for the rest of the morning.

Whatever.

There was a golf cart with my name on it.

Once Tom and Lilly left, it was time to get to work. Equipped with a trash bag in one hand and my Three-Day Notices in the other, I ventured out into the wind and—*wowza!* Good thing I had the extra pounds to keep me anchored, or I'd be flying over Santa Monica. Einstein broke loose and swirled around in front of my face, sticking to my glossed lips and poking at my eyeballs.

In the first courtyard, Daniella was on all fours again, examining the lawn. Her glasses were on the tip of her nose, lips pursed, nose scrunched, dark hair flying, little fingers parting blades of grass.

I stood over her, fighting the wind to say upright. "What are you doing?"

"Get off, or you'll kill him!" she yelled at me, in both English and Spanish.

I jumped off the grass. When Daniella barks, you moved.

She poked.

"Are you looking for the dog poop?" A Domino's Pizza flyer smacked me in the face.

"No. I lost Gary."

"Who?"

"My *Grammostola pulchra*," she said, as if it were obvious.

"Is that Spanish for a dog?"

She looked at me as if I were stupid. "No, it's my tarantula."

*Tarantula?* My subconscious summoned imaginary spiders to crawl up my back, and down my legs, and across my neck. "Is it...um...big, black, and furry?"

She went to her knees and removed her glasses. "You see him?"

I scratched my back and legs and neck and...*ahhhhh!* "I think so. He was in...my...bed." I shivered.

"You slept with Gary!"

"No! He crawled into my bed this morning."

"He crawled into her bed?"

I heard whispers from above. Gloria and Tam from Apartment 7 were on the upstairs walkway in their bathrobes.

"You saw Gary!" Daniella was now in front of me. "Did you kill him?"

"She killed Gary," Gloria echoed in a stage whisper.

"I didn't kill anyone...*ouch!*"

Daniella jabbed me in the arm with her finger—a bad habit of hers.

"You kill my *Grammostola pulchra?*" she said.

I rubbed my bicep. "Why don't you say tarantula instead of gramma-*blah-blah*? And stop poking me."

She jabbed me again. "You kill him?"

"No, I didn't kill him. He escaped, and we looked everywhere but never found him." I held my hands up to fend off another finger attack.

"What?" She wrestled with her hair whirling around her face. "Gary cost 150 dollars, and I have that bill for you."

"Gary must be a prostitute?" Gloria now had a bag of low-fat white cheddar popcorn.

"Makes sense," Tam added.

"No, he's not. For the last time, we're talking about a spider!" I yelled up to the cheesy-fingered duo.

"He's my emotional pet," Daniella said to them.

Gloria propped an elbow on the railing. "How do you get an emotional pet?"

"It's easy. You get the certificate online, and then she pays for it." Daniella cocked her thumb in my direction.

"No, I don't pay for anything. Why would I pay for your emotional pet?" I pulled a pine needle out of my mouth.

"I need an emotional pet," Gloria said.

"No, you don't," Tam quickly amended.

"I've always wanted a Great Dane." Gloria waved a chip around. "You could take the dog on your runs," she said to Tam.

Tam cut his eyes to me, but I didn't say a thing. Again, it wasn't my place to insert myself into residents' personal relationships.

It was, however, my job to insert myself into a conversation that involved the purchase of a 100-plus-pound dog.

"You can't get an emotional pet without a note from your *doctor*," I said.

"That shouldn't be a problem." Gloria dusted off her fingers. "My dentist lives here. He's cool. Will that work?"

"No." *I don't think?*

Daniella dug her finger into my arm again.

"*Ouch*! Stop doing that!"

"I need to get into your apartment and look for Gary." A CVS ad slapped her in the face. Half-off Easter candy.

I peeled it off her and shoved it into my trash bag. "I'll come get you after my meeting, and we can look for Gary. Trust me. I don't want him hanging out in my apartment any more than you do."

"OK, and you can give me my reimbursement when you're done too."

"I'm not paying for your spider."

"It's the law."

"No, it's not."

"Yes, it is."

"No, it's not."

"My cousin is a lawyer, and he said so."

"Lilly's father is an attorney, and he said I am not monetarily responsible for your pet." *Note to self: double-check this over with Tom.* "He also said stabbing me with your finger is considered assault with a blunt weapon. Would your cousin like to speak to my lawyer about these charges?" *So there.*

Daniella puffed her chest.

I puffed mine.

She glowered.

I glowered.

She opened and closed her mouth, then pounded off. *Aha!*

I'd successfully rendered Daniella speechless. Me! I almost couldn't believe it. A huge victory. Residents came to me all the time with *My lawyer this…My lawyer that…My lawyer says laws don't apply to me…My lawyer says I don't have to pay late fees…* If Tom was going to sleep in my bed and eat my Girl Scout Cookies and tell our daughter he had a sparkle present for me and kiss me and run away and…I forgot where I was going with this?

*Spider…dog…finger jab…video games…* Right, lawyer.

If he was going to string me along, then I was going to use his law degree.

Now, on to my golf cart.

To get there, all I had left was:

—Deliver Three-Day Notices

—Pick up a landfill's worth of trash.

—Find the dog poop.

*Err…never mind.*

—Change shoes.

* * *

For every piece of trash I picked up, another two took its place. You'd think the trustee wouldn't hold Mother Nature against me. But Trevor was also a McMill, so it was a crapshoot.

Mr. Nguyen came from the second courtyard with a plastic trash can and a rake slung over his shoulder. He strolled along the pathway as if he were on a jolly holiday.

"Good morning," he said cheerfully. "When the trash truck came this morning, they knocked over the bin. I got the third courtyard. Now I take care of this. You go do what you need to."

"Thank you!" I said into Mr. Nguyen's ear and handed him the trash bags. "I have to deliver these notices. If you need me, my phone isn't working, so call me at the office."

Mr. Nguyen shooed me off. "Go, go. And don't worry."

Having a responsible, hardworking, all-around remarkable maintenance man was the best gift any manager could have.

I ran to the second courtyard, squinting to keep debris from entering my corneas. This wasn't the warm windstorm typical for this time of year. This was a cold blast of air hitting exposed skin like 35-mph daggers. Of all days for California to deviate from its typical weather patterns.

Four residents had failed to pay their rent. I ran around and shoved notices in Apartment 3's, 12's, and 31's doors. The apartments weren't in numerical order. Why? I had no idea. The original architect was probably high or had a wicked sense of humor, because it was annoying. The last stop on my Pay Rent or Leave tour was Apartment 15. Even after our conversation, Shanna never did come in for a copy of her lease, nor did she drop off a check or money order. It wasn't a good sign when a resident defaulted on their second month of tenancy.

The door to her apartment was wide open. I knocked and poked my head in. The living room was bare of any furnishings. No couch, no television, no pictures on the wall. Nothing. This was also not a good sign.

I thought back to my interaction with Shanna the day before. She'd appeared on edge, asked for a copy of her lease, said she didn't get the job she'd auditioned for. Crap! She'd skipped. Of all days to bail on your lease, she had to choose today.

Frustrated, I shoved the Three-Day Notice into my pocket and inspected the damage. The bottom halves of the wall were a little dirty. The carpet was dotted with stains. The kitchen cabinets looked untouched, but it smelled like pickles. She'd left behind a sink full of dirty dishes, food in her fridge, and one dining chair.

The apartment wasn't too bad. But it would cost more than the 500-dollar deposit to return it to a re-rentable state. Not to mention lost rent.

Patrick was going to flip.

I scratched my neck and moved to the bathroom, taking note of the broken toilet seat and cracked mirror. "Honestly. You couldn't have waited until tomorrow?" I scratched my nose.

When I could no longer open my right eye, I realized— cat.

Shanna had a cat.

I knelt down and ran my hand along the carpet. There was enough fur to make a sweater, matching hat, and scarf. It felt like I had two habaneros shoved up my nasal septum, and all I wanted to do was rub my face against a cactus.

But before I could, a scratching and whimpering sound came from the master bedroom. I froze mid-sneeze.

*Did she forget a cat?*

*Do cats whimper?*

I hadn't spent much time around a cat since my mom bought me a kitten when I was eight. You know, guilt present. *Sorry. Your dad and I couldn't make it work. Here's a cute little kitten so you don't feel so bad. Oh wait, you can't breathe? I'm going to take it back now.*

It was no wonder I had issues.

Frantic, I followed the whimpering through the apartment. My vision blurred with each step. Inside the closet was something fuzzy. I picked it up and retreated, fast, before I keeled over.

# CHAPTER SEVENTEEN

———

*See also: Pet Sitter*

I was wrong.

Shanna did not have a cat.

I had in my arms some kind of Chihuahua/bat/rabbit half-breed I was pretty sure was a dog. It was as round as it was long, with little legs, wiry hair, and a stub for a tale. He (or she) wiggled around, kicking his legs like he was swimming, which made the trek back to my apartment difficult. It was like holding an energetic watermelon.

Once safely inside, I fell against the front door and slid down to my butt. The dog licked my face. "Poor little..." I lifted it up to take a peek. "Guy." I sneezed, wheezed, coughed, and sniffled.

The dog stared at me with bulging brown eyes. Hurt my heart. He was so ugly he was almost cute, but what was I supposed to do with a dog? I already had an urn and a tarantula to deal with.

I'm telling you, this property management gig is no sissy man's job. That's for sure.

Also, how do you forget a dog?

Urn, fine. You were in a rush. It was in a box. It didn't currently have a pulse, you forget. But a dog?

Unsure of what else to do, I made a bed out of princess towels and left a bowl of water in Lilly's bathroom. "It's too windy on the patio. You'll blow away," I explained to him, in case he took issue with his accommodations. "And there's too much stuff in my bathroom."

He sat on his right hip and panted.

"I have an important meeting, so I'll need you to hang out here quietly, and do…whatever it is dogs do…" I unfolded the copy of *Daily C-Leb Mag* on the floor, the one with Jessica Wilders on the cover. "When you have to use the restroom, please do so here."

The dog sniffed at the paper.

"We'll figure out what to do with you after the meeting. But I can't keep you, so don't try any cute dog stuff."

He batted his bulging eyes at me.

"I said don't do anything cute. This is a no-dog-or-cat property, and I can't breathe around you."

He whimpered.

"Fine. I'll pet you, but that's it."

I took a knee and scratched him under the chin. He kicked his back leg. If only every guy in my life were this easy to please. "OK, enough of this. I have to go." I stood and looked around. "I suppose you'll need food. What do you eat?"

He scratched at my shoe with both paws.

"I mean, yes, you eat dog food. But I don't have any." *Achoo!* "Do you like quesadillas?"

\* \* \*

It turns out dogs don't like lactose-free whole-wheat quesadillas. Or turkey sandwiches on rye. Or Cheerios. Or Top Romaine. But they do enjoy frozen Marie Callender's Pot Pies. This whole dog thing was a foreign undertaking. I'd never owned a pet in my life. It brought back the same I-don't-know-what-I'm-doing-and-I'm-about-to-freak-out feelings from when I first had Lilly.

I went ahead and handled it the same way I did then. I called Mrs. Nguyen, crying.

"You sure that's a dog?"

We stood at the bathroom door, leaning against either side of the doorjamb, watching the little pooch. He was taking a siesta on Jessica Wilders' face. This was after he peed on his bed.

"I think he might be a Chihuahua mix?" I said.

"What's with the music?" She pointed to the radio on the counter. An old boom box I'd dug out of the storage closet.

"I thought music would help pass the time for Munch." I'd chosen the country station. Munch struck me as a country music type of a dog. Not sure why. Could be the hair.

"Munch?" Mrs. Nguyen said. "What is a munch?"

"He's Munch."

"Munch what?"

"His name is Munch. The least I could do was give the poor dog a name instead of calling him *dog*. Detective Munch is my favorite character on *Law & Order SVU*."

"You watch too much television."

"So I've been told."

Mrs. Nguyen grabbed my cheeks and squished them together. "You look bad. Why you so red?"

"I'm allergic to animals," I said through fish lips. "Typically, I only have this bad of a reaction to cats."

She released my cheeks. "So why you keeping it?"

"I'm not keeping him. But I don't know what else to do until the meeting is over. Look." I closed the door, and Munch went ballistic. Barking at an ear-deafening octave. "His deadbeat owner left him in a closet, and I think being in here brings back painful memories."

"You can call animal control," she said.

"Shhhh. Don't say that in front of him. I need to look into it. To be sure he goes to one that won't—" I leaned in. "K-i-l-l him. Can you watch Munch until the meeting is over? Just be sure he doesn't bark. Please?"

Mrs. Nguyen rolled her eyes. "Fine. I'll stay here with that thing. But go put makeup on. You look terrible."

\*   \*   \*

After I reapplied my makeup, I sat at the desk and fretted, angling my stapler just so, arranging my pens in the cup, restocking my business cards and brochures. I had half an hour until Patrick and Trustee Trevor were set to arrive, and I was a snotty, red-eyed, blotched-face, wheezing mess with a tarantula on the loose and a dog hiding in my apartment. Which could prove problematic should Patrick or Trevor have to pee. The pool bathroom had been converted into a storage unit sometime before my reign. It was a good thing I never did get around to buying water bottles.

What I knew about the McMills was pieced together from conversations over the last few months. I knew their history with their son Kevin. I knew they owned half a billion dollars worth of properties around Southern California. I knew they were old. I knew they did not like dogs or cats. On page one of The House Rules it said: *No cats or dogs permitted. Caged animals only with Landlord's permission.*

For the record, I never gave Daniella permission to buy Gary.

*Bah-haha-haha-haha*

From what I understood, this was on every lease on every property they owned. Patrick said they were unyielding when it came animals.

So now I had a dog.

Feeling both jittery and pooped (*hello, Benadryl*), I continued to fuss around my desk, rearranging all non-consequential items like the tape dispenser, paperclip holder, and the razor-sharp letter opener. I'd cut myself on that thing more times than I could count. I re-pounded the reports into a neat stack, placed them in front of *Mom*, and took a pause.

I wondered if Trustee Trevor would ask why I had an urn on my desk, and once I told him, if he'd be impressed with my care of both current and ex-residents and their deceased loved ones—or find it absurd. I couldn't ignore the fact my life had been a series of unfortunate events since the moment I placed *Mom* on my desk.

Maybe this was why Steph had yet to claim her? What if her mom was a crazy ax murderer who slew villages, and now I had her?

Except, who used an ax to murder this side of WW II?

Or lived in a village?

Also, I didn't believe in all that paranormal stuff.

I put my chin in my palm and studied the urn—the light reflecting off the glossy surface, the dark swirls along the grain, the curved edges, the tiny scratch from when I knocked it into the telephone. Even with the blemish, it was pretty. As far as urns go, it resembled a miniature coffin. I picked it up and looked underneath to see if there was a sticker for the mortuary. No sticker, but another engraving, this one into the wood itself.

*Katherine M. Roberts*

*July 3, 1974–August 4, 2003.*

The name and birth date didn't sound right. I grabbed Steph Woo's file and found the photocopy of her driver license. She was born in 1984. Katherine Roberts would have been ten years old when she had Steph.

Unless I had misread the year of birth?

I blew on the wood and polished it off with a tissue.

*Nope, still 1974.*

I called Steph. "You've reached my voicemail. I'm not available right now." I lip-synced her greeting. "Please leave a message!"

I didn't bother. I'd already left four. I ran my finger down her original application and stopped at the emergency contact.

*Name: Jennifer Woo*

*Relation: Mother*

Oh hell.

On an impulse, I flipped to her employment verification. Steph was a teacher at a preschool in the valley. I dialed the number and placed the phone up to my ear.

"Early Start Preschool, this is Leah," answered a springy voice. Children sang and chuckled and cheered in the background.

"Hi. I need to speak with Steph Woo, please," I said.

"She's in class. Can I take a message?"

"No," I said with conviction. No more messages. "I'm her apartment manager, and it's important that I speak with her now."

"Is everything OK?"

"It's about her mother."

A part of me hoped she'd retort with, "But her mother died when she was seven, and Steph changed her birthday so she would appear younger." Otherwise, whose mother did I have on my desk?

"Oh no. Let me go get her."

Crap.

An instrumental version of ABC's came on until Steph picked up. "Hello?" I heard the panic in her voice, and I felt guilty.

"Steph, it's Cambria Clyne, your old apartment manager."

"Hi, what's wrong?"

"Did you listen to any of my voicemails?"

"I haven't yet, why?"

Honestly, what was the point of voicemail? "I called because I have your mother."

Silence…

"*What?*" she finally said. "Why do you have my mom? Is this because I painted the walls? You better not hurt her!"

"No. I have your mother's urn," I added quickly.

"My mother's urn?" she cried out. "What did you do to my mom?"

*Well, this had escalated quickly.*

"Nothing. I found an urn in your carport. It says *Mom*, and I assumed it belonged to you since it was in your cabinet."

"Whaaaaa?"

"Did you have anything in your carport cabinet?"

"Yeah, but I cleared it out on Monday night. I never had an urn. Messing with urns that don't belong to you disturbs—"

"The deceased," I finished for her. "What time did you end up leaving Monday night?"

"I left around six."

"Then why did you have me meet you for a move-out inspection Tuesday morning?"

"I thought I'd be back, but I got stuck in traffic…" Her voice trailed off. "I'm at work," she said, as if just remembering. "Is there anything else?"

"I don't think so," I said.

We hung up, and I rubbed my temples. So we had a killer running around, a tarantula crawling around, and a dead mother on my desk.

Tom was right.

This did sound a lot like an episode of *Ghost Confidential.*

# CHAPTER EIGHTEEN

———

*See also: Urn Sitter*

There were too many freaky things happening over the last forty-eight hours.

My worst-case scenario mind thought the murders, Amy the urn, the car accident...were all somehow connected and I might not live to see my next birthday!

My logical mind thought, *Calm the hell down and take another Benadryl.*

So I did.

Better.

*OK. Let's start with the urn.*

I googled *Katherine M. Roberts July 3, 1974–August 4, 2003*. An article from the *San Fernando Valley Chronicle* came up.

*Katherine M. Roberts, 29, was found dead at her apartment on Monday, August 4, of a drug overdose. One child was found in the apartment.*

*"We find overdose scenes more and more these days. This one was particularly difficult because of the child who had been inside with her mother for at least a few hours," Lt. Josh Jaspen, Chief of Detectives, said on Tuesday morning during an interview on the local radio station, Valley News 540-AM. "We received the call from Roberts' ex-boyfriend, who found her dead, beyond any life-saving measures, when he'd brought their 14-year-old daughter over for a visit. It's a terrible situation."*

*When asked what would happen to the 7-year-old, Lt. Jaspen said, "She is currently with Child Protection Services and doing as well as can be expected."*

Well, crap.

*What am I supposed to do with this information?*

I drummed my fingers along my forehead—to help the thinking process along—when in my periphery I noticed Mickey standing outside the window staring at me. He had on a gray T-shirt pulled tightly over his belly, leaving an imprint where his navel was. For a man who spent most of his day walking around, he was rather plump. Dark stains circled under his armpits, and his pants were faded camo print with dirt on the knees. I liked Mickey. I had no reason not to. He paid his rent on time. Didn't cause problems. Was pleasant. But he was freaking me out. Just standing there. Staring at me.

Unsure of what else to do, I waved.

Mickey didn't.

I squirmed in my seat and mouthed, *Hi.*

Nothing, like someone had pressed Pause and he was stuck mid-stare.

I grabbed a pen and pretended to be busy. Hoping he'd leave. But, nope. There he was, standing there, staring at me.

"Do you need something?" I asked through the window.

Mickey didn't reply. Instead, he titled his head to the side and squinted at me until I realized, *Where did the screen go?*

I pushed away from the desk, walked through the lobby, and opened the door. The wind was still blasting through the property, and I made a visor with my hand. Mickey had disappeared. I peeked into the carports, into the laundry room, and checked behind the mailboxes by the lobby door.

No Mickey.

He was gone.

Just like the window screen.

*Weird.*

A missing window screen seemed like something I would have noticed, especially with the inspection coming up. And if I didn't catch it, no doubt Mr. Nguyen would have. I turned around, about to go find Mr. Nguyen, when I saw that the screen on my apartment window was barely hanging on. The aluminum frame was so badly bent it could snap in half with minimal pressure, like someone had hastily pulled it from the window and couldn't get it back on.

*Huh?*

On a hunch, I walked back into the lobby, through my office, opened the door to my apartment, and inspected the window from the inside. The locking mechanism was loose, and the window was ajar an inch, not enough for anyone to get in, obviously, but it explained why the wind had whistled so loudly that morning.

Someone had broken in to my apartment.

But who? And, why?

I spun around in a slow circle. There was nothing of value in there. Even my television was an old boxy unit. Nothing appeared to be missing. Unless…it dawned on me that Tom had not set my apartment alarm the night before. The office alarm, however, had been on, and the keypad for both was in my kitchen.

Someone first tried to break into the office, saw that the alarm was on, and thought they'd go through my apartment instead. Made sense. It was rent day. I had thousands of dollars sitting in the safe. Of course, all were personal checks and money orders made out to Elder Property Management, except for the illegible money order. Which was made out to scribbles. And I never kept cash.

Unless whoever attempted to break in wasn't going for the money?

I walked into the office and took a seat. There was not much of worth in there either. The computer was old. The answering machine originated in the '90s. There was the fax machine. Not sure anyone but Patrick used the fax system anymore. The shredder? Mom? Keys to an apartment?

My eyes cut back to *Mom.*

The urn had to belong to someone there. Otherwise, wh would it be in the carport? Would that *someone* break in to get it?

It was an absurd notion. It wasn't as if I were holding th urn hostage. A simple *hey, can I have my mom back?* would suffice.

But if there was one thing I'd learned during my short stint as an apartment manager, it was never to discount the most ridiculous option. People rarely used common sense.

My head was too foggy to figure this mess out on its own. I grabbed a pen and a pad of paper. *I'll try this whole "think on paper" thing*, I thought.

*I have the urn of Katherine Roberts. Katherine Roberts had two daughters. Someone attempted to break in to my apartment. Could it be one of the daughters? Katherine Roberts. Roberts...Roberts. We have two tenants with the last name Roberts who live here. Tam Roberts in Apartment 7 and Shanna Roberts in Apartment 15...no relation to each other...Roberts is a popular last name...but Shanna Roberts did skip. Her carport is next to carport 17...*

Could I have Shanna's mom on my desk? And did she attempt to break in to get the urn before she bailed?

# CHAPTER NINETEEN

———

*See also: Just a girl standing in front of her boss asking him not to fire her*

The lobby door chimed. I nearly jumped out of my seat—so on edge. It was Patrick. Right on time.

Patrick Elder was a middle-aged, no-nonsense type of guy, with a cul-de-sac of hair and a love of checkered shirts and the phrase "don't hold your breath." He removed the sunglasses from his face, hooked them on the collar of his shirt, and had a look around.

I sprang upright. My chair crashed into the filing cabinet behind me.

"Don't say it." Patrick raised his arms as if about to fend me off. "Don't say we have a problem. I was with Trevor McMill at our Burbank property yesterday, and it didn't go well. Too many vacants. The grounds were a mess. The energy was off. We found a resident had snuck in a dog. Trevor fired the manager on the spot." Patrick flung his briefcase on the counter. "I don't get paid enough to work with the McMills."

I wasn't sure how to respond, so I didn't. The Burbank problems sounded an awful lot like my problems. And no matter how crazy my job was—and it *was* crazy—I wanted to keep it. Why? I didn't know. Maybe I was crazy too.

"Sorry." Patrick pinched the bridge his nose. "It's been a rough week of visits. Traffic is a nightmare. This wind is bizarre. Go ahead and tell me—Yikes. What happened to your face?"

"I, eerrr…" I just realized there was Kleenex shoved up each nostril. I plucked the tissues out and tossed them into the trash.

Judging from the deep parallel lines across Patrick's forehead, it was not a good time to bring up the dog hiding in my apartment, the skipped rent, how I believed Shanna broke into my apartment to get her dead mother who was on my desk, and, oh yeah, there was a giant tarantula around here somewhere.

"It's allergies," I said instead.

"The wind?"

"Sure."

"Everything else OK?"

"I've got it all under control." *Kind of...not really.*

Actually, not at all.

Patrick unloaded his briefcase, slamming folders onto the counter, one at a time—muttering something about the rock salts of life? I'd never seen him so flustered.

I pulled my phone from my back pocket and held down the Power button.

*Please turn on. Please turn on. Please turn on. Please turn...yes!*

I composed a quick text to Chase: *I think a resident tried to break in to my apartment last night. Call me.*

But before I could press Send, the screen went black.

*No!*

The front door flung open, and in came a lumberjack-looking man. He stepped inside and struck a Superman pose with his hands on hips, feet parted, chin pointed to the ceiling. He had on denim overalls, cuffed at the bottom to better show off his moccasins, and a red flannel shirt, cuffed at the sleeves to better show off the rope bracelets tied around his hairy wrists. His thick black-rimmed glasses were two sizes too big for his face, and his beard was big and poufy and looked as if it were constructed of pubic hairs. It matched the man bun on the top of his head.

*This can't possibly be...*

"Trevor!" Patrick took on an uncharacteristically jovial tone. "Welcome." He extended a hand, and Trevor stared at it but didn't move. Awkward. Patrick cleared his throat. "Glad you made it. This is Cambria Clyne, the on-site manager here." He made a sweeping motion, as if presenting royalty.

*You can do this*, I told myself. I had to appear normal and friendly. "Hi. I'm Cambria—"

In came Mickey, mumbling to himself, something about corrupt cops and cats. He walked between Man Bun McMill and me. We waited for him to pass. I took another breath and started over. "Hi. Nice to meet you." I kept my hands to myself.

Trevor stared at me with a businesslike frown. "Cambria Clyne," he said slowly.

My eyes went from Patrick back to Trevor. "Yes?"

"Cambria!" He kissed me on each cheek and gave me a hug.

*OK?*

Trevor held me for much longer than California Labor Code permits. My arms were plastered to my side, and my cheek was pressed up against his. He smelled like granola and garlic, and his pubey beard scratched my cheek. Once released, he kept his hands on my shoulders and his face close. Really close. Too close. I counted six blackheads on his forehead.

"Cambria, you have a beautiful aura," Trevor said.

"Thanks?"

Trevor McMill's gray eyes bored deep into mine. I was half weirded out and half intrigued. "Don't doubt yourself," he said in a yoga instructor voice. "You are a natural leader with good instincts. Trust them."

So Trevor McMill was a walking fortune cookie. Didn't see that one coming. "A lesser soul would have abandoned this place months ago. You persevered. Brava." He clapped his big, hairy hands together in slow motion. Patrick half-heartedly clapped along.

A standing ovation?

This was going suspiciously well.

"You do yoga, right?" Trevor asked.

"Once." When I first moved to LA. Pretty sure that was requirement before you were allowed to have a 310 area code.

"I can tell. Now." Trevor clicked his tongue. "I want to hear all about the plans for the lobby." He rubbed his hands together as if he were at an all-you-can-eat buffet.

Patrick and I shared a look. We'd yet to discuss the design plan. The insurance adjuster hadn't even been out yet. Heck, the air scrubbers and hydroxyl machines were still purring.

Trevor tossed an arm over my shoulders like we were two longtime chums. "I see orange. Orange says 'Live here. Rent here. Be here. Exist here.'"

"Yes," I almost sang. "An orange accent wall behind the couch, then a soft gray for the other walls."

"Add in a pop of blue," said Trevor.

"What about small palms on either side of the couch to go with the LA vibe?"

Trevor nodded along, seeing my vision. "We need a fountain. The living waters of life adds to the peacefulness of feng shui."

"Sure."

"A mirror above the couch to disperse the light."

"And steel accents."

Patrick's eyes bounced between Trevor and me like he was a tennis official. Patrick's favorite color was neutral. All this talk of pigment must have given him anxiety. The reason the lobby had remained untouched for so many years was because, as much as Patrick Elder hated color, he hated spending money more.

"We'll need to cleanse the space before we add life." Trevor shook his finger playfully at Patrick. "Have you read the article I sent you on the living salt waters?"

Patrick blinked.

"Hold one moment." Trevor placed his fingers to his temples as if he were receiving a telepathic message. "There is something off in here."

I looked around. Aside from the fact the walls were missing, everything appeared in order, except for Gary, who was crawling across the counter. That freaking spider was on my last nerve.

"I can sense it," Trevor said.

I ran my finger around my collar.

Trevor backed up and was about to lean against the counter… "No! Not there!" I grabbed his arm and yanked him away.

Patrick looked like he was going to barf.

"You should, *um*, stand over there." I steered him to the corner. "You can feel the essential wellness of the salts better from here."

Trevor regarded me through a cautionary glare before he said, "You're right." He pointed to the spot beside him. "Stand, Elder."

Patrick did as told.

"Close your eyes and feel with me."

Patrick first rolled his eyes then closed them.

I agreed. He didn't get paid enough.

Gary was headed for Patrick's briefcase. I could not believe I was about to do what I was about to do. It took every ounce of willpower I had to guide the hairy tarantula onto my shaking palm. His little legs were spikey against my skin and tickled up my forearm.

Certain situations were beyond profanity.

This was one of them.

"I'm sensing an unbalance," Trevor hummed.

*Me too.*

I escorted Gary to the office. It was one of my worst nightmares realized. Soon my teeth would fall out, and my pants would disappear, and I'd be back in high school, sitting next to a seven-foot clown.

"It's a disturbance," Trevor said with his eyes still closed

I ushered Gary into an empty copy paper box and quietl stabbed the lid with a pen to make breathing holes.

"There's a hurt soul trapped in here. You feel it, Elder?"

I glanced at *Mom*. Holy hell.

"No," said Patrick.

*OK. I might be a believer now.*

I plopped Gary next to *Mom* and rushed over to Trevor. "What do we do about the unsettled spirit?" I asked him.

"Salt."

"Salt?" I repeated in wonder. "What do I do with salt?"

Patrick grumbled.

"Salt," Trevor continued, still studying the inside of his lids. "It must be placed in all four corners of the room to rid the disturbance. I sense it's a woman…she's crying for her…children."

*Note to self: Go to Costco. Get a flatbed cart. Buy all the salt.*

"Why is she crying?" I asked.

Trevor drew in a breath. "She's upset about…there's been a disturbance…"

"Is it because I moved her? Would she rather me put her back in the carport?"

Patrick sighed. I imagined him thinking something along the lines of *I work with morons.*

Just then, Munch barked. He had great vocals for a little dog.

Trevor's eyes shot open.

Much barked again.

Oh geez.

Trevor's eyes narrowed. "Was that a…dog?"

"I have reports!" I said. "Reports! Reports! Reports!" I dashed to my desk and grabbed the reports. I heard Mrs. Nguyen muttering in Vietnamese behind the door.

I let out a nervous chuckle. "Here…here you go." I handed Trevor the folder and noticed for the first time the stick figure drawing on the back. Lilly and me under a rainbow, holding hands, both with squiggly hair and triangle dresses on.

Munch howled.

"There it is again. What is that?" Trevor asked.

"*Um*…my upstairs neighbor, Mickey, he's…singing."

"Didn't he just walk through here?" asked Patrick.

*Thump! Crash! Bark!*

"How about a tour of the property?" I ran to the lobby, yanked the back door open, and let in a gust of leaves. Some landed on the floor—most went on Trevor.

He pulled a pine needle out of his beard and dropped it on the ground. "It's a co-mmu-ni-ty," he said, accentuating each syllable. "We don't have *properties*. We have co-mmu-ni-ties."

*Bark!*

"Ahhhhhh!" I didn't know what else to do. So I yelled.

Patrick's mouth dropped open.

"Ahhhh'mmmm so happy you're here," I sang, mortified. "Let's go, shall we?"

The three of us stepped outside. The courtyard was sprinkled with leaves and pine needles, but no trash. Mr. Nguyen was a miracle worker.

My phone buzzed from my back pocket, and I stole a glance. It was Chase. "I need to take this," I said, excusing myself.

Patrick shot me a look of disbelief. "Now?"

"Go ahead. We'll wait," said Trevor.

*Errr…OK.* I took a step closer to the mailboxes and plugged one ear to hear over the wind. "This is Cambria. How may I help you?"

"It's Chase."

"Oh hello, sir."

Patrick and Trevor stared at me. I covered the receiver and said "prospective resident" to the two men. They both nodded approval.

"Cambria, are you in trouble?"

"I'm in a meeting right now. But the…*um…*" *Mind blank. Mind blank.* "I have that information for you in my office. Can you hold on one moment, sir?" I buried the phone in my uniboob and gave the men a manufactured smile. "I'm sorry, but I have a prospect who is eager to rent here. I'll be right back." Before they could protest, I ducked inside and closed the door behind me. "Chase, are you OK?"

"I'm here. Curious…I'm here with a…new…Shanna Roberts…last month…what do you know…a Michael Smith."

"Chase, my phone is broken. I'm going to lose you."

…

"Chase?" I looked at my screen. The call was still connected. "What about Michael Smith? What about Shanna? Chase? Hello? Crap."

I swallowed back a lump of panic—but it bounced right back up. Chase had said "Michael Smith." I was sure of it. He had also said "Shanna Roberts." Chase had no idea Shanna Roberts had skipped. Michael Smith was connected to Jessica Wilders somehow, but how was Michael Smith connected to Shanna Roberts? And if both Jessica and Shanna were connected to Michael Smith, did that mean they were somehow connected to each other?

And since I knew Shanna and I had her mother, did that mean *I* was now connected to Jessica Wilders?

Maybe the worst-case scenario portion of my mind wasn't so wrong after all?

# CHAPTER TWENTY

———

*See also: Defender*

I soared past plans A thru C and landed on D.

Plan D: Rub temples and bite at lip until Patrick knocks on the window, taps his imaginary wristwatch, and tells you to get outside.

When I opened the door, Trevor and Mr. Nguyen were forehead to forehead. "You have a blue aura," Trevor said.

"Cambria is back," Patrick announced. "Time to get a move on."

The wind had dwindled to a breeze, and we walked along the pathway in the first courtyard, through the ivy-laced breezeway, and past the pool. Trevor must have said "wow" and "amazing" a dozen times during our journey, pointing to everything from the blooming flowers to the clean railings. If I weren't wading through a smog of panic, I would have burst with pride. As it was, I had to make a conscious effort not to wet myself.

Had I gotten myself mixed up with Jessica Wilders and what press was now calling the *Ghost Confidential* Murders?

"Have we ever had a resident by the name of Michael Smith?" I asked Patrick under my breath while Trevor inspected a bush.

"I can't remember the name of every resident we've ever had at all the properties…I mean *communities*. Why?"

I shook my head. "Nothing."

While Trevor and Mr. Nguyen chatted about water consumption, I peeked into the third courtyard to make sure Kevin wasn't out and about and nude.

No Kevin, but Trent in Apartment 23's tight-pant brunette had arrived. She performed her balancing act up the stairs. She waved to Larry, who was on his upstairs balcony vaping, and to Silvia, who was in the doorway yelling at her parrot, Harold, on her shoulder.

"Smoke will kill Harold!" Silvia berated him from her doorway.

Larry puffed out a cloud of smoke with a devilish grin on his face. The situation was exaggerated by Silvia, who had on a baby-blue nightie turned see-through by the sunlight, and Harold, who had on a diaper.

*They make diapers for birds?*
*Who knew?*

I was getting quite the pet education today.

"I'm calling management." Silvia slammed the door.

My phone buzzed from my back pocket.

*Ignore.*

Trevor stuck his face up to mine, and I went cross-eyed. "I can see Kevin's door is still black?"

"Yes. But we did fix the window," I pointed out. "Now that's he's back, I can speak with him about painting the door if you like. I was told he had more flexibility since he's the owner's son."

Trevor looked taken aback. Unfortunately, he didn't take any actual steps back. "Kevin is home?"

"He's home?" Patrick mirrored Trevor's shock. "Why didn't you tell me Kevin was back?"

To be honest, I didn't think it was that big of a deal. But instead of saying that, I said, "*Ummmm,*" because I have a way with words.

"The agreement was that he goes to rehab. A short prison sentence won't work," Trevor said.

"As far as I knew, he was sentenced to three months in prison and then rehab," said Patrick.

"If he didn't do rehab, then he can't live here." Trevor cleaned his glasses with the sleeve of his shirt. "If he didn't keep his end of the deal, then I don't keep mine."

Mr. Nguyen made himself scarce by inspecting the ground.

"Kevin can't leave," I said. "Isn't three months in prison good enough? He did rehab last year, and it didn't work. I think prison might have had a bigger impact. He looks better and is acting normal."

Trevor peered through his giant glasses to be sure all spots were gone before he shoved them back on his face. "Rehab gives him the tools required to stay clean. Prison gives him more contacts to buy drugs from when he gets out. We went through this before. I thought he had decent representation. What idiot lawyer would get a drug addict out of rehab?"

He did *not* just snub the experienced and dedicated Thomas J. Dryer, Attorney at Law. I was about to go all Silvia on him, but Patrick said, "We could have him pay rent" and saved me from myself.

"If he wants to live here for free, then he has to follow my…I mean…his parents' rules. I realize he had a taxing childhood. My aunt and uncle are old-school souls. But he's over forty years old now. At some point you have to take accountability for your own actions…" Trevor drew on and on, but something about the phrase "taxing childhood" stuck with me.

*A taxing childhood…*

Where had I heard or read this before?

I thought back to the picture of Jessica on the front of *Daily C-Leb Mag*. Her deep-set brown eyes. The article. *Taxing childhood.*

Jessica, Shanna, Michael Smith…

*…Jessica and Shanna and Michael Smith…*

*Jessica and Shanna and Katherine and Michael Smith and a taxing childhood?*

"Cambria!" Patrick snapped his fingers in front of my face.

I gazed at him.

"What do you think about our idea?" Patrick asked, trying to sound polite, but I could tell by his face he was irritated.

I stared at him. "Idea?"

"What is going on with you?" he hissed under his breath

"We're going to have Kevin pay rent," Trevor said. "At a discount, but if he defaults, he's out, just like every other resident."

"But he's not like every other resident," I said. "His parents agreed he could stay here for free so long as he doesn't contact them. Why should he be punished because he suffers from addiction? As a McMill, as the *trustee*, shouldn't you look after the well-being of not only the com-mu-nity but also your cousin? Addiction is a disease. We should be helping him, not hindering him. He needs support. Having him pay rent now when he just got out of prison is a terrible idea. It's the opposite of what you should be doing." Though Kevin paying rent would help my bottom line…quite a bit. But still. Kevin and his parents had an agreement. Right was right. And while I wasn't allowed to say anything about the cheaters and secret gamers around here, I could stick up for Kevin.

Patrick pulled at the few hairs he had left on his head.

Trevor pressed his eyebrows into a *V*. "You're bold, Cambria Clyne. You're wrong, but you're bold. I like you. Kevin pays rent. Let's move on." He waved for the group to follow then swung an arm around Mr. Nguyen's shoulders. "I'd be curious to hear your take on what the energy of this place is."

My phone buzzed. It was Tom. He must have gotten a new phone. The call dropped before I could answer. The phone buzzed again. It was a 310 area code, and, once again, the call dropped before I could answer. My voicemail notification lit up, but I was unable to access it.

I followed the group of men, my mind still churning over how Shanna Roberts and Jessica Wilders were connected. Shanna Roberts, *Katherine* Roberts, Jessica Wilders.

The little light bulb in my head turned on.

Jessica was twenty-eight the day she was murdered. Which meant she was born in…*carry the one…add the two…*

The little light bulb in my head reminded me that my phone had a calculator, except I couldn't access my calculator. So I resigned myself to using my fingers…*add the two…*Jessica would have been fourteen.

Fourteen!

Could her childhood have been "taxing" because she had an addict mother? An addict mother whom she found dead of a drug overdose when she was merely fourteen years old?

If that were the case, then would that make Jessica and Shanna sisters?

# CHAPTER TWENTY-ONE

———

*See also: Snoop*

"I have to go!"

The three men whirled around. Somewhere under his beard, Trevor's mouth was agape. Mr. Nguyen looked concerned. Patrick shot me a disapproving frown before saying, "Where could you possibly have to be right now?"

"It's an emergency." I fumbled the keys out of my pocket and juggled them around. "Here. Go look at the vacant apartments." I tossed them to Patrick. They bounced off his face.

*Note to self: you have the world's worst aim.*

"If it's an emergency, then we'll accompany you," said Trevor.

"It's not that kind of emergency. It's...*personal.*" I left the last part open for interpretation.

No more questions asked.

I couldn't tell them that I thought Shanna Roberts'—who, oh yeah, skipped on her lease—sister was the super-famous and super-dead Jessica Wilders, and I was pretty sure I had their cremated mother on my desk, because I'd sound crazy. And maybe I was crazy. Maybe Tom was right. I had turned an innocuous situation into an episode of *Law & Order*—or better yet, *Ghost Confidential.*

Mr. Nguyen plucked my keys off the ground and handed them to me. "I have my master key. You go ahead."

Poor guy looked confused.

Patrick and Trevor rocked on their feet, unsure of what to say next when Mother Nature did me a solid and diffused the situation. The wind returned and blasted our exposed skin with tiny blades of debris at record-breaking speed. I held up my hand to protect my eyes.

Trevor's man bun came unraveled, and his hair waved around him as if he were Pocahontas singing about the colors of the wind.

Patrick covered his eyes and hunched over in agony, while Mr. Nguyen yelled, "Let us go see Apartment 17!"

"Good idea!" Trevor fought with his mane to get it back in place. "Let's go inside."

I tugged on Mr. Nguyen's sleeve. "Take them to the other vacancy if they breeze through that one quickly," I said.

He nodded. "No problem. Everything OK?"

"We'll see."

I ran to the office as fast as I could, which wasn't fast at all, more like an excited shuffle, because I was out of shape and...well, I was out of shape. I'd officially squashed any hope of a golf cart. At this point, I hoped for a job when this was over. I hoped I wasn't in prison for harboring a celebrity's dead mother when this was over. Heck. I hoped I wasn't dead!

I took a seat behind my desk, shook the mouse to wake up my computer, and googled *Jessica Wilders' mother.*

*Birth Name: Jessica Katherine Wilders*
*Place of Birth: San Fernando Valley, CA*
*Parents: Jerald Wilders (56) and Katherine Roberts (deceased)*

My head imploded.

The urn on my desk belonged to Jessica Wilders. I'd found it Tuesday morning, hours after she'd been murdered.

The question remained: why was it in Apartment 17's carport cabinet? Something told me Steph Woo had nothing to do with it. The close proximity to Shanna's carport was too great of a coincidence.

Without warning, the computer screen went black. "No, no, no! Not right now, please." I shook the mouse. "Turn back on, please?" There was no use. The power was out.

Technology was really screwing me over.

My eyes cut to *Mom.*

Fine.

I leaned in close, cupped my hands around my mouth, and whispered, "What is it that you want?"

She didn't answer back. Thank goodness, because things were already too paranormal for my taste. I swiveled around in my chair and rolled to the filing cabinet, pulled Shanna's file, and flipped to her application.

*Name: Shanna Katherine Roberts*
*Age: Twenty-One*

I punched the numbers into an actual calculator because I didn't trust my fingers. In 2004 Shanna was seven years old. Jessica was fourteen, and Shanna was seven. Now I was sure of it—Shanna Roberts and Jessica Wilders were half sisters. I had their mother on my desk and not a clue what to make of this situation.

I called Chase but was unable to get through on my piece-of-crap cell, and because the power was out, the office phone didn't work either.

It was time to take matters into my own hands. I excitedly shuffled to Shanna's apartment and opened the door. Nothing had changed. Not that I expected it to. I cracked the living room window in hopes that fresh air would stifle the allergens.

No such luck.

It felt as if a pair of imaginary hands were wringing out my lungs. My eyes filled with tears, my throat itched, and my nose was a free-flowing faucet of snot. It wasn't pretty.

Wasn't pretty at all.

The one-bedroom apartments are 800 square feet with two walk-in closets, a hall linen closet, and an open kitchen plan, filled with cabinets. This was a lot of space to cover in the short amount of time I had left to breathe.

I threw open the kitchen cabinets, one by one, in search of what? I wasn't sure. All I knew for sure was Shanna and Jessica were sisters and I had their mother. Someone attempted to break into my apartment the night before, and Shanna disappeared that day.

Coincidence?

Methinks not.

I feared that (A) Shanna was involved with her sister's murder, or (B) Shanna had been murdered.

Though Hampton said the killer didn't break in. He shot from the outside, Rambo style. It seemed unlikely the killer would steal Shanna's home furnishings. It also seemed unlikely someone so ostentatious would break into my apartment by removing the screen. Which meant it was probably Shanna coming in to get her mom.

But this was all a theory. I hoped there was something left behind to debunk it. I didn't want to be mixed up with Jessica Wilders more than I already was. People around her were dropping dead by the minute.

And I wasn't in the mood to die that day.

Nothing was left in the cabinets aside from a plastic bowl and a dirty *Keep Calm and Act On* mug. The bathroom cabinets were bare except for an extra roll of toilet paper. The master bedroom was bare. I opened one of the closets, and out came an orange tabby cat. He rubbed his body against my leg and purred.

*Will there be a new animal every time I open a door?*

"Sorry. I can't pet you," I said to the feline. "If you could go somewhere else, that would be great."

The cat stretched his front legs and yawned. Then he walked to a slice of sunlight on the carpet and lay down.

Inside the closet, a white linen shirt hung on a velvet hanger. There was a litter box on the floor, along with a scratch post. If I had use of my nasal septum, I was sure it smelled awful. I patted my hand around on the top shelf and found a white paperclip that looked to have been painted over when the apartment was turned. That was it.

The door for the water heater cabinet was ajar. I was able to access the flashlight on my phone to take a peek. Behind the 30-gallon tank was a weathered shoebox that once held pink sneakers, kids size 12. I lifted the lid and found a stack of letters, a dried rose, photos, a Barbie, and a cheap plastic charm bracelet with a variety of seemingly inconsequential charms: a baby bottle, wrench, anchor, guitar, dog, cat, bird, toothpaste.

I pulled a picture from the stack. It was a woman with dark brown hair and deep-set brown eyes. Her cheeks were sunken and her hair thin. She was sitting on a webbed lawn chair with a beer in one hand and a cigarette pressed between her lips. There was no date or name on the back, but I had a sinking suspicion this was Katherine. She had the same eyes as Jessica and Shanna. The next picture was Katherine with two little girls. I recognized one instantly as Jessica. The gap-toothed smile gave it away. She looked to be around eleven years old, while the other girl seemed to be about four. Katherine stood with a hand on each of her daughters' shoulders. Both girls had matching plastic charm bracelets around their wrists—the same one that was in the box.

The stack of letters was bound together by a rubber band. Most were still sealed. On the front of the pile was a letter addressed to *Jessica Wilders* with a Los Angeles address, sent in 2009. *RETURN TO SENDER* was stamped on the front. I counted twenty-seven letters in total. All but three were sealed, with the *RETURN TO SENDER* stamped in big, hard-to-miss red lettering.

I slid an opened letter from the stack. It was from Jessica to Shanna. A single sentence: *Stop writing me.*

In the back of the bundle was a white paper folded into thirds. It was an email from Shanna to Jessica. I scanned the message. The cat hair in the air caused my vision to blur, but from what I was able to read, Shanna was desperate to connect with her older half sister, but Jessica did not want to pursue a relationship.

I felt a tinge of heartache for Shanna. Her mom had died when she was seven years old. Per the article, she sat with her dead mother for at least a few hours and was then sent to foster care, while Jessica went with her father. I'd be crushed if my sister wanted nothing to do with me. Not that I had one. But I could imagine.

It didn't mean that Shanna had anything to do with Jessica's death though. Maybe she was so overcome with grief that she moved. Or maybe she chose this apartment because it was close to Amy Montgomery, Jessica's on-set rival, giving her easier access to plant incriminating evidence in her car.

*Gulp.*

Also behind the water heater was a well-worn spiral notebook. The front and back covers were ripped and faded. The spiral wire that looped around the side was misshapen and inflexible. Many of the pages were smeared beyond legibility, and what wasn't smeared was scribbled writing.

A flyer for the Animal Center for Chance Adoption Fundraiser slipped out and fell to the floor. On the front of the flyer was a picture of Jessica holding...*Munch*?

I wiped my eyes with the back of my hand and looked closer. It was Munch alright. There was no mistaking that face. I thought back to what Amy had told Chase, how Jessica had been upset about what had happened at a fundraiser she'd had over the weekend.

The cat returned and rubbed up against my back. I shooed it away and wiped my eyes to read better. The fundraiser was the week before at The Grove and promised special appearances by Jessica Wilders *and* Lance Holstrom. I shook the notebook, and out fell adoption papers for a terrier mix and an orange tabby cat, which Shanna had adopted at the fundraiser.

I conjured up the scene in my head. Jessica and Lance were there to promote animal adoption. They were surrounded by pens filled with dogs and cats in need of a home, along with a dozen security guards. No doubt their presence drew a crowd. *Ghost Confidential* was a hit television show, and Frank and Lola were the Derek Shepard and Meredith Gray of the paranormal romance world. Everything was going well. Dogs and cats were off to good homes. Lance and Jessica posed for pictures with the newly adopted animals. Then here comes Shanna. She had her new dog and cat with her. She wanted her picture taken with Jessica and Lance as well. But Jessica wanted nothing to do with Shanna. She called security to have her removed. Shanna caused a scene. Maybe she cried, screamed, kicked, told everyone her sister had emotionally abandoned her. People gathered around, confused as to why Jessica Wilders, who was known for her love of animals, was being so mean to this poor young woman, who'd just adopted two animals.

Of course, I could be completely off. But my gut told me I wasn't. Still, it didn't mean Shanna killed her sister.

A picture from last season's cast of *Ghost Confidential* fell out of the notebook and landed at my feet.

Both Lance and Jessica had an *X* etched over their faces.

*OK, so it looks like we're going with Theory A.*

I opened the notebook. Pasted to the inside cover was an email from Jessica sent one month ago.

*Shanna,*

*Please stop contacting me. This is bordering harassment. You're lucky I haven't called the police yet. I will not give you pointers for your acting career. I will not have lunch with you. I will not let you have the urn. I do not want to pursue a relationship. Please keep your distance. If you contact me again, I will have you arrested. No one in the family wants to deal with you.*

Well, there was a motive. Shanna wanted a relationship with her big sister. Her big sister didn't want a relationship with her. And Jessica had the urn. How it ended up in Steph's carport was beyond me.

I took a picture with my phone and tried to send it to Chase, except, of course, it wouldn't go through. *Freaking Tom!* If he hadn't scared me, I wouldn't have dropped my phone, and I would have spoken to Chase earlier, and I wouldn't be sitting in a pile of cat hair. I lifted my phone above my head, as if that would help—like being closer to the satellite would make it work.

For the record: it doesn't.

I sent him a text message instead.

*I'm in Shanna Roberts' apartment. 15. She is Jessica Wilders' sister. It looks like she might have had something to do with Jessica's murder. You should come quick.*

I hit Send but was unsure if it went through or not. With a sniffle, I continued to flip through the notebook. Pages and pages of nonsensical ramblings. Shanna had blamed Jessica for her going to foster care. She was jealous of her sister's acting success. She blamed Jessica for her inability to land an acting gig. The more I flipped, the messier the writing became, until I made it to the last page. There was something about a cousin Shanna was unable to reach. Written on the side margin below *I hate Jessica,* was written *Cambria Shampoo.*

I squinted and re-read it. *Cambria Shampoo!*

What did she do to my shampoo? And there was a checkmark. Good thing I hadn't washed Einstein in...*Sunday...Monday*...four days.

*Note to self: throw away all hair products.*

*Sub-note: throw away all beauty products to be safe.*

*Sub-sub-note: Throw away everything. Shanna was in my apartment!*

Or maybe that was why she broke in to my apartment. To get my shampoo?

Freaking Tom. I knew I should have set the alarm last night.

That man was really on my hit list.

I took pictures of everything and felt around behind the water heater to see what else might be back there. I pulled out a black flip phone, a T-shaped wrench, a box of gloves, and a funnel.

I gasped. *Tom's car!*

Clearly this was a crime scene, and I had to keep it credible by not touching anything. Except I'd already touched everything. But no one had to know that. I shoveled all the papers back into the notebook and stuck everything behind the water heater, when my hand landed on something leathery. I pulled out a wallet. Not just any wallet. It was Tom's wallet and his phone!

I couldn't believe Shanna had left so much incriminating evidence behind before she moved. It was like she'd wanted to get caught. If it were me, I would have burned it all before I moved. Chase did say there were stupid killers, but this seemed...too stupid to be true.

*Oh no.*

A thought trotted into my head. With a gulp, I opened the notebook and flipped to the last page. It was written in sloppy, nonsensical, heartbeat scribbled writing. Like the money order...for...the...one...bedroom. Crap!

# CHAPTER TWENTY-TWO

———

*See also: Intruder*

My heart heaved. Shanna didn't skip. She didn't move. Shanna paid her rent. The wind must have blown her door open. I was currently breaking and entering.

One could make the argument that she was breaking the law more. But this wasn't a competition. The apartment might have been empty of furnishings, but she did pay her rent, and I had no right to be in there. Shanna still had possession of the apartment.

I scrambled to my feet, stumbled backwards, and stepped on the cat's tail. He hissed.

"I'm sorry," I said.

The cat didn't accept my apology and rubbed his hair along my leg.

My body felt as if it was stuffed with cotton, except for my head. My head was heavy. Like it was stuffed with rocks. And my chest burned. I staggered down the hallway and ran my hands along the wall to keep myself upright.

The front door opened, and Shanna walked in with a bulging reusable grocery bag in her hand. She looked about as shocked to see me as I was to see her.

"What are you doing in my apartment?"

"There was a…" *Think. Think. Think. Think.* "Leak!" I almost sang, impressed my weight-filled brain was able to conjure up such a good lie on a whim. "There was a leak, and I had to get in here right away. I left you a message."

Shanna looked at her phone. "I didn't get it." She pressed her brows together. "You don't look so good."

"Allergies." I coughed. "You know, the wind."

Her eyes darted around the room. "How'd you know there was a leak in my apartment?"

That was an excellent question.

I sneezed. "Water dripped from the ceiling below."

"Oh…yeah…makes sense…" She paused to adjust the bag in her hand. "Did you…um…fix it?"

"Yeah, it was a faulty…pipe. Faulty pipe. All is well now." I had no idea if she was buying it or not. My right eye had swollen shut.

"Did you go in the closet?"

"Just the bathroom. I better get going. My boss is outside waiting for me."

"Oh…yeah…OK…um…cool." She went to the kitchen, opened the fridge, and unloaded her groceries like nothing was amiss in her world.

I blinked my left eye a few times, coughed twice, and walked out of the apartment, trying not to appear rushed. If Shanna wasn't suspicious, then I should be able to make it back to the office before she realized Munch was gone and I'd been in her closet.

What I failed to take into account was that my body was made of cotton and that the closet would be the first place Shanna would look after I left.

I made it as far as the pool before I heard the footsteps fast approaching. Shanna grabbed the cutout in the back of my shirt and pulled me to the ground. "It's against the law to enter an apartment and go through the tenant's things," she said, standing over me.

"I thought you had moved. The door was wide open," I said in a panic.

"Why would I move?" She took a seat on my chest. "You took my dog, and I know you have my mom on your desk. I saw her through the window when I went to pay my rent. Why do you hate me so much? I never did anything to you."

"I don't...I don't hate you." I gasped for air. "I didn't know the urn was yours. I found it in the carport and thought it belonged to Apartment 17."

Shanna peered down at me. "So go into my apartment and look through my stuff?"

"I...I didn't. It was a..." Oh hell. This wasn't going to end well for me. Not when I was stuck under Shanna's bony butt. I punched her in the stomach, and she fell over.

And Tom made fun of me for watching *WWE*.

Shanna landed on her back and kicked me. I kicked her. We did this for a while, me kicking her, her kicking me, until she grabbed hold of my leg and dragged me toward her. We rolled into the pool fence, and I was able to get on top of her.

"Did you kill Jessica?" I asked her.

"I didn't kill anyone."

She spat in my face and pushed me down. Gross.

We rolled again, her on top of me, me on top of her. She clawed at my face. I clawed at hers. I'd never been in a physical fight before, and I had a hunch neither of us was doing it right. We wrestled for the upper hand until we rolled into the pool. Under the water Shanna was able to break free. I kicked to the surface, wiped the chlorinated water from my eyes, and watched Shanna climb out.

I doggy paddled to the ledge and hoisted myself up and out of the pool. Shanna stole one glance back then took off running. I chased after her, all the while begging my legs and lungs to hold on for me. My soaked clothing didn't make the situation any easier. I was more than fine letting Shanna run away, but she was headed right for the office, and I wouldn't allow her to hurt Mrs. Nguyen. I grabbed hold of Shanna's waist, and the two of us landed in a bush. Einstein clung to a thorny branch while Shanna was able to get up. She bolted into the lobby.

I scrambled free and rushed after her. Shanna grabbed the urn from my desk and tucked it under her arm, like a drenched football player about to run in for a touchdown. She snatched the letter opener and held it up.

"Don't take another step," she said.

I held up my hands. "If the urn was so important to you, why did you put it in Apartment 17's carport?"

"It's none of your business. Now, where's my dog?"

I didn't want her in my apartment. "He's staying at a friend's house. I'll call and have him returned."

Shanna shook the letter opener at me. Her makeup dripped down her face, and her eyes were encircled in black smudges from her mascara. "No. You can take me to him. I want my dog so I can get out of here," she said.

I was feeling a little weird, standing there dripping wet, being held at letter-opener-point by a woman, also dripping wet, with an urn tucked under her arm. Pretty sure an episode of *Ghost Confidential* started this way.

Confession: I hated the show. I only watched because Amy was on it, and I fast-forwarded to her parts. Had I known I'd be starring in my own real-life episode, I would have not only watched, but taken notes.

I was hoping to distract Shanna with conversation and create an opportunity to snatch the letter opener away. That sucker was sharp. It could easily penetrate an organ or two. She didn't look comfortable holding it, which begged the question of whether she was capable of holding a gun and shooting someone.

"You don't have to threaten me with office supplies," I said. "I never wanted the urn to begin with, and I'm allergic to animals. I have no problem giving either back."

Her eyes welled up. "Yeah, but you think I killed my sister."

"Are you sure you didn't?"

"I'd never hurt anyone."

"You threw me on the ground, and now you're holding a sharp object at me," I pointed out.

"That's different. You went through my apartment. I heard you were nosy, but I never expected you to be a criminal."

"Where did you hear I was nosy?"

"On Rent or Run dot com. Also, you have sex with old people."

I rolled my good eye. "You can't believe everything you read on the internet."

Shanna's hand trembled, and she blinked back tears. "No, you can't believe *everything* you read. Jessica was a horrible person who treated me like dirt, but I didn't kill her."

I caught a glimpse of motion outside the window. It was so fleeting I thought I'd imagined it. "If you didn't, then who did?" I asked Shanna.

"Why…why don't you ask your friend, Amy Montgomery? She hated Jessica. Everyone knew it."

"Yeah, that ship has sailed. The police know someone planted evidence in her car."

Shanna's lower lip trembled. "I…I don't know what you're talking about."

The door leading to my apartment opened, and Chase appeared with his gun drawn and pointed at the back of Shanna's head. "Drop your weapon," he said.

Shanna let go of the letter opener, and it fell to her feet.

"Put down the box, and put both hands in the air," Chase ordered.

Shanna set the urn on the desk and raised both hands high above her head. "I didn't kill anyone," she said with a whimper. "It wasn't me. I'm not a murderer."

"We'll talk about it at the station." Chase cuffed Shanna.

Hampton came running in. The two men worked in unison. One patted her down while the other read her the Miranda rights. I took the opportunity to fall to the ground and curl into a ball.

Hampton directed Shanna out the back lobby door. She maintained her innocence the entire time. If I hadn't read the notebook, I would have believed her.

To be honest, I had no idea what to think.

Chase helped me to my feet and pulled a twig out of Einstein. "Are you hurt?"

"Probably." I was too pumped full of adrenaline to feel any serious injuries.

"Why are you wet?" Chase asked.

"I fell into the pool."

"What happened to your face?"

I touched my puffy eye. "Allergic reaction."

"To the dog that's in your apartment?"

"It's Shanna's dog. Did you see Mrs. Nguyen in there?" I asked.

"I sent her and the dog into your room for safety," he said.

I shivered, and Chase disappeared into my apartment and returned with a beach towel. Luckily, it wasn't the one I'd used for Munch's bed. He wrapped it over my shoulders and rubbed them to bring back the warmth.

"Did...did you get my text?" I asked through chattering teeth.

"I'm here, aren't I?" He smiled.

Good point.

"Pretty sure my phone is officially dead. I dropped it this morning, and it was in my pocket when I fell into the pool."

"Did she push you into the pool?"

"No. We were fighting and landed in there."

Chase looked heavenward and sighed. "So I have this straight," he said. "You somehow ended up in Shanna's apartment with a notebook, and you think she killed Jessica. You two got in a fight. Ended up in the pool, and Shanna's dog is with Mrs. Nguyen."

"That's a fair synopsis of the situation."

"How did you end up in her apartment?" he asked.

"I thought she'd moved out."

"How did you end up with her dog?"

"I thought she'd moved out."

He pointed to *Mom*. "And the urn?"

"I thought it belonged to a move-out."

Chase thunked the heel of his hand against his forehead. "You kill me."

"I-I appear to have that effect on men."

He gave me a curious look. "Huh?"

"Never mind." I coughed, sneezed, sniffled, scratched my face, and shivered.

"You should take something for the allergies."

"I'm already maxed out on meds."

Chase cut his eyes to the window to be sure no one was watching. The coast was clear. He wrapped his arm around my waist and kissed me. "I'm glad you're not hurt." He went back to rubbing my arms.

Warmth returned to my limbs, enough that my teeth stopped chattering.

"Did you know the entire time that Shanna and Jessica were sisters?" I asked.

Chase shook his head. "We found out yesterday. Not public knowledge, but her assistant told us. This isn't Shanna's address though. She has a studio in downtown, but we saw that Elder Property Management had run a credit and background check on her last month, which didn't make sense. That's why I called you. To see if you remembered her coming in and filling out an application. We were talking to her apartment manager when I read your text. When I got here, I saw her holding you at knife point."

"Letter opener," I said. "So basically what you're saying is that I solved this case for you."

"Nothing has been solved yet. And I thought I told you to stay out of it?"

"I did…until I didn't. You're welcome."

Chase thunked his forehead again. "This is far from over. Stay right here, and don't touch anything. I'll be right back."

I agreed and watched Chase walk out to the carports through the window. My body felt all jittery, and I fell to the chair and put my face into my hands. I was already feeling the adrenaline letdown when the door chimed. Patrick, Trevor, and Mr. Nguyen walked inside.

"That was a wonderful walk-through, Mr. Nguyen. Thank you." Trevor stuck his finger in his ear and gave it a wiggle. "Very loud and very thorough. Attention to detail. That's what I like."

"It's what we strive for." Patrick looked at me and made a face.

I imagined I looked about as awful as I felt.

"Did you go for a swim?"

I had no words. Patrick was clueless, utterly clueless as to what just happened. I shared a glance with Mr. Nguyen. I owed him a cake, or a hug, or more overtime, or a kidney, or something.

"No, I fell in," I said. My eyes went from Trevor to Patrick. Their expressions were unreadable. "I was helping a resident?"

A smile spread across Trevor's face, and he looked at Patrick. "I like her. She's dedicated."

That was one word for it.

"Cambria, I have to apologize," Patrick said. "Mr. Nguyen told me you were in a car accident last night. Is that what you tried to tell me when I got here?"

It was still baffling that they had no idea what had just happened.

"Yes," I finally said to Patrick.

"And your emergency…" said Trevor, giving me the once-over. "You all *good*? 'Cause your face looks a little…big."

"I'm fine now, thank you." I forced a smile.

"Well then, folks"—Trevor clapped his hands, and I jumped—"I think I've seen just about everything. Looks great." He held up his fist.

*Am I supposed to fist bump him?* This man was a walking conundrum with a bun. I couldn't figure him out.

I hit his fist with mine.

"*Nice*," he said. "I better be off so I don't hit traffic."

Patrick held the door open for everyone.

"Come on, Cambria," he said, his voice unyielding.

"*Um.*" Chase told me not to move, but OK.

We walked Trevor to his Prius parked at the curb. "Cambria, it's been a pleasure to make your acquaintance." He kissed me on each cheek. "I like this one," he said to Patrick as I weren't there. "She's quick, and the place has never looked better. And you." He made little pistols with his fingers and aimed them at Mr. Nguyen. "You are the essence of the salt of life. Am I right, Patrick? Or am I right?"

"Sure."

"Make this man a maintenance supervisor," he declared

"We'll look into it," Patrick said.

Mr. Nguyen blushed.

"Now I must be off," said Trevor for the tenth time.

"I'll see you tomorrow in Long Beach." Patrick held his hand out, and Trevor swatted it away.

"None of that. Come here." Trevor pulled Patrick in for a hug.

I'd never seen anyone look more uncomfortable in all my life. Patrick, not Trevor. Trevor had the face of a man who'd just found a toilet after holding his pee for ten hours.

As Trevor drove off in his silent car, the three of us stood at the curb and waved goodbye with smiles plastered to our faces.

Once out of sight, Patrick snapped his head around so fast I thought it was going to fall off. "What happened today? You're lucky your aura is so salty, or whatever the hell Trevor says, and you're even luckier Mr. Nguyen took over for you. I understand you were in a car accident, but you should have told me this morning instead of disappearing like that. And I don't understand why you're all wet."

Before I could respond, a parade of police cars came flying around the corner—both marked and unmarked. News vans from every station I'd ever heard of, and some I hadn't, pulled up behind them.

"We have a slight problem," I told Patrick. "Jessica Wilders, the actress. Well, it looks like Shanna Roberts from Apartment 15 may have had something to do with the murders."

Patrick stared at me as if I were speaking a different language then asked, "Didn't we do a background check on her?"

"Yes, we did, and her record was clear. Unfortunately, background checks don't include 'yet-to-be-carried-out premeditated murders.'"

Mrs. Nguyen ran out with Munch in her arms to see what the fuss was about. "What is happening?"

Patrick looked as if he were waking from a daydream. "Why do you have a dog?" he said to Mrs. Nguyen.

"It's not a dog. It's a monster with legs. Here." Mrs. Nguyen shoved Munch into my chest. "This dog has the countenance of my great aunt Ly."

"He belonged to Shanna," I explained to Patrick.

Patrick blinked and shook his head. "Wait one moment. You're saying Shanna Roberts in Apartment 15 is the one who killed that actress with the gap teeth? The one who's all over the news?"

"That's the one," I said.

"She was too skinny," added Mrs. Nguyen.

A police officer pulled crime scene tape across the carports, and a group of paparazzi congregated behind the trees with their cameras covering their faces.

"Cam!" Tom pushed through the crowd and nearly knocked a reporter to the ground. "Cam!" He had one arm up and was waving. "Cam!"

"Mom, we got a dog?" Lilly cheered.

"No. No dog." I handed Munch to Mr. Nguyen. Who gave him to Mrs. Nguyen. Who gave him to Patrick.

"Cam, what happened?" Tom put Lilly on the ground and hugged me. I buried my head into his chest and inhaled him. Who needs essential oil when you have a Tom? "You're not going to believe this," he said. "But someone did drain my oil and replace it with water and loosen my power steering pump valve. You were right. It wasn't an accident."

I readjusted the towel around my shoulders. "Can you say that again?"

"You were right…" His smiled faded, and he had a look around. "Why are there so many cameras here?

"It's a long story."

# CHAPTER TWENTY-THREE

———

*See also: Adult Daycare Provider*

The com-uuu-nity was alive with the sound of police activity. Yellow tape blocked Shanna's door. Yellow tape blocked Spencer and Amy's apartment. Residents were talking to reporters. Paparazzi were climbing the fence. Police people in uniform, and detectives with gloves and bags in their hands, walked around. CSI. FBI. *TMZ*. Everyone was there. Police were in the storage unit. Police were in the office. Police were in my apartment. K-9 units sniffed out the property. It was mayhem.

Mayhem, I tell you!

Patrick, Tom, and I all stood in the second breezeway looking out at the chaos. Lilly was with Mr. and Mrs. Nguyen in their apartment with Munch. Amy and Spencer were still at the Ritz. Her agent told her to stay away from the scene and let the cops search her apartment to be sure no other evidence had been planted in there.

Amy was in the middle of a seaweed wrap to help her cope with stress. There wasn't enough seaweed in the Pacific Ocean to help me with mine.

I hoped Amy's close connection to the crime wouldn't backfire. But looking around at the police coming to and from her apartment, and the army of paparazzi circled around the property, I wasn't so sure the narrative to this story would sway in her favor.

The three of us walked to the third courtyard. Sophie from Apartment 38 was on the upper walkway, taking video of the police in Amy's apartment.

Great.

We took a seat at the picnic table. I crossed my arms on the tabletop to make a pillow for my aching head. I closed my eyes and let wind hit my face. I'd yet to change my clothes, but Tom had given me his sweatshirt, so at least I was warm...*er.*

We sat in silence until I was hit in the head by a shoe. I looked up at the second-story walkway. Alexis from Apartment 23 was throwing Trent's clothes over the railing.

"What are you doing?" Patrick yelled up to her.

"My husband is a pig." She hurled six hangers filled wit dress shirts over. "He's a two-timing pig!"

Patrick turned back around. "I'm not touching that."

Throwing clothes into the courtyard had to violate at least one of the many house rules. Littering? Keeping common areas clean? Not acting like a lunatic in public? Though that wasn't a rule. But it should be an addendum.

Sophie now had her phone pointed at Alexis. "He's a pig!" She hurled his Xbox over the edge.

Tom ducked out of the way.

*Yeah, OK. I guess I should deal with this.*

Tom worked to save the Xbox by picking up the loose pieces scattered around the grass. Patrick remained mum. I was able to stop Alexis before she threw the television over.

"Please don't discard your personal property in the courtyard," I told her.

Alexis's eyes swam with tears, and her face turned red. "You knew, didn't you!" she screamed at me.

I held my hands up. "I don't get involved with my tenants' personal lives unless it affects the safety of others," I said. Thank goodness for that.

Alexis frowned, and she looked at the thirty-inch plasm in her arms. "Can I throw this in the dumpster?"

"If you don't want it anymore, and it fits, then you're more than welcome to."

She flipped her hair and marched down the stairs. I hea the crash of the television meeting the dumpster. Outwardly I cringed. Inwardly I laughed. Not that it was my place to say anything but—served him right.

I went back to my spot at the picnic tables. "Is she moving?" Patrick asked.

"I suspect he is."

"Maybe you could rent him one of your vacant apartments?" Tom suggested with a wink, obviously kidding.

There was enough drama around here without inviting exes to live next to each other.

"I like the way you think, Tom," Patrick said. "Except, I do have a bone to pick with you. Kevin. Why didn't he do rehab?"

"That was against my recommendation. So Kevin ended our professional relationship via email last month."

"You never told me that," I said.

"Attorney-client relationship. I couldn't." Tom shrugged. "Why? What's going on with him?"

There was a loud *clump...clump...clump...*and we all turned to the back stairwell. Kevin dragged a large painting down the stairs. It was Van Gogh smoking a joint in front of a *Starry Night*. Kevin stopped to wipe his brow with the backside of his hand and then dragged it to the dumpsters. He returned a moment later with the television and a pair of Nike shoes.

# CHAPTER TWENTY-FOUR

———

*See also: Press Secretary*

Munch chased his butt until he ran into the wall. In another life he must have had a tail. I wiped my nose with a plush bath towel. Kleenex wasn't cutting it. My lungs no longer hurt, both eyes were open, and I was told my face didn't resemble a tomato anymore. It appeared I was far more allergic to the tabby cat than Munch. Good thing, because he was rubbing his body up against every surface in my apartment.

I carefully lowered into a chair at my kitchen table and cracked open a Cherry Coke. "Can you hand me the vanilla?" I asked Tom.

He dug into the reusable grocery bag and pulled out a pint of Ben & Jerry's vanilla ice cream. I plopped a scoop into my cup and poured the Cherry Coke on top. It was almost magical how ice cream could cure most everything—except my back, and my ribs, and my sternum, and my shoulder, and every muscle in my entire body.

Aside from that, I felt better.

Tom had bought everyone else dinner from the Mexican restaurant around the corner. A Ma-and-Pa place called Mexican Food Restaurant (why mince words?). It was the type of hole-in-the-wall establishment only locals dared try. The abundance of homeless men, women, and prostitutes meandering the sidewalk scared the tourists away. Mexican Food Restaurant had the most authentic Mexican food in the area. Granted, I'd never been to Mexico. Tom had. He said it was authentic. So I went with it.

Lilly ate her taco, and Tom had a burrito the size of my head.

"What'd you order again, Kevin?" Tom asked.

"I got the chicken quesadilla and beef tamale." Kevin had come over to…I wasn't sure why he came over. But he was there, on the other side of my table, eating a quesadilla.

Mexican Food Restaurant had better quesadilla-making skills than I did.

"Today was fun. My favorite part was the pretty yellow tape." Lilly picked the lettuce off her plate and put it on the table. "And I love mine's new puppy!"

I scooped the lettuce into her taco. According to Tom, authentic tacos didn't have lettuce, but I had requested she have at least one vegetable on her plate. Lettuce was Tom's idea of a vegetable.

"It's *my*," I told her. "And like I said, we can't keep him. This is his temporary home." Until I heard from Chase or Hampton what to do with Munch, I let him stay in my apartment. Which was fine. He was cute, and breathing is overrated.

"What's temporary mean?" Lilly asked.

"It means not permanent," Tom said.

"What's not permanent mean?"

"It means the dog belongs to someone else," Kevin said.

"Oooohhh." Lilly took a bite and gave Munch a piece of lettuce.

He chewed on it for a while then spit it out on my shoe.

I took a sip of my Cherry Coke float, leaned back in the chair, and looked out the window. After five hours of pure chaos, the community had calmed. Only a few paparazzi remained, and the police tape had been removed from the office, storage unit, and Amy's apartment. Hampton and a female detective I'd never met before had interviewed me for over an hour. I gave them a play-by-play of how I came to find Shanna's notebook and box of letters. Hampton said if he didn't know me, he wouldn't have believed me.

Not sure if that was a jab or a compliment. I took it as the latter.

The power was back on, cell service had been restored, and all was right in Southern California again. I heard the hashtag #cellmagedon was trending on Twitter during the hour that service was down. The wind had slowed enough for a helicopter to report from above, and the rhythm of the blades beating in the air had become our new ambiance. I was scared to turn on the news. I was scared to go outside. *Daily C-Leb Mag* had called the office six times asking for a statement.

What was I supposed to say?

*We now have three one-bedroom apartment homes available. Defense attorney included in rent.*

Honestly. I was beginning to wonder if this place was cursed. Or maybe it was me?

What I knew for sure was that I'd never touch an urn again. Not that I believed in all that...*that* much.

There was a knock on the front door, and Chase let himself inside. He paused in the middle of the living room when he saw Tom, Kevin, Lilly, and me gathered around the table, eating our authentic food.

"Did you see my new temporary puppy?" Lilly asked Chase.

"I sure did." Chase took a knee and scratched Munch on the head. He excitedly beat his stub on the carpet—the dog, not Chase.

Tom took a bite of his burrito, and Kevin leaned over. "Don't worry. You've got a solid fourteen pounds on the cop," he whispered. "You could take him."

Tom frowned down at his midriff and put the burrito back on the plate.

I mentally slapped my forehead.

"Are you hungry?" Kevin asked Chase.

"You can have mine's green stuff." Lilly held up a string of lettuce between her thumb and forefinger and made a face.

"I'm good, but thank you for the kind offer." Chase winked at her, and she blinked both eyes back. It was their thing. And it was adorable.

"You need to eat it, Lilly," I said as firmly as I could muster. "All of it." It was the only nutritional element to her dinner. Over the last twenty-four hours she'd had a horrible diet—donuts, Slurpee, quesadilla, and who knew what Tom had fed her when they were out. My guess was McDonald's. I was feeling like a crap parent. Not to mention we had, *once again*, been harboring a dangerous criminal in the apartment building. This was becoming a semiannual thing. I was overcome with parental guilt. And her eating the lettuce would make me feel better.

I looked to Tom for backup. He nodded. I nodded back.

"Give it here, Lil." Tom took the taco, pulled all but three pieces of lettuce out, and handed it back to her.

She stared up at her daddy like he was Superman.

*Note to self: work on nodding communication with Tom.*

I swigged the last of my Cherry Coke float and poured another.

"Cambria, can I talk to you privately?" Chase asked. He was still petting Munch.

Munch had rolled to his back, giving Chase access to his stomach. His little eyes were rolled back into his head, and his tongue wagged. The dog, not Chase.

I *slowly* got up from my seat, followed Chase outside, and stood under the upstairs walkway to hide from the helicopter hovering above us. He closed the door and hugged me. I wrapped my arms around him and dug my face into his chest. I was happy my nasal septum was no longer clogged, because Chase smelled good. He had a sexy man scent. A musky mixture of salty skin with a hint of soap. It was intoxicating.

"I'm sorry," he said.

I peered up at him. "It's not your fault."

"I should have kept a closer eye on this place." Chase cupped my face with both hands. "Why does it feel like trouble always finds you?"

"I'm beginning to think I'm cursed."

He gave a half-hearted laugh, as if I'd told a joke, but I was serious. "How about I take the dog so you can breathe better," he said.

"How about you take the urn and put it back at Jessica's house."

"Done. And I'll take the dog too."

I sniffled. "What will you do with him?"

"He'll go to a shelter to be watched temporarily until Shanna is released or charged."

I blinked back the allergy tears. "She isn't charged yet?"

"As of right now, she's looking at possible charges of brandishing a weapon."

"A letter opener," I corrected.

"Anything is a weapon if you turn it into one."

"Fair enough. What about the stuff found in her closet?"

"CSI is taking a look at it now," he said.

"Do you know if she's the one who tried to break into my apartment?" I asked.

"We haven't interviewed her yet. We're waiting for her attorney to arrive." Chase wiped away the tear running down my cheek. "Let me get the dog away from you."

I grabbed hold of his forearm. "No. Leave Munch. He's been through a lot of stress today. You can take the cat."

"What's *Munch*?"

"The dog. I named him Munch."

"I think his name is Rover."

I rolled my eyes. "Unoriginal. Munch is better."

"Isn't that the name of the detective you like on *Chicago PD*?"

"*Law & Order SVU*. Detective John Munch. But you can call him Munch."

Chase let out a laugh and kissed me. "You keep Munch for now, and I'll talk to my supervisor about what to do with him. Why don't you get some rest and…" He scratched the back of his head. "How long is *he* going to stay here?"

"Kevin?" I played coy. "I'm not sure. Why?"

Chase tilted his head. "You know who I'm talking about. I realize he's going to be around. I'm just curious for how long, that's all."

"I don't know. His car is totaled, so I'll have to take him home, I'm sure."

Chase's brows snapped together. "What happened?"

"Tom and I were in a car accident last night. Someone, aka Shanna, drained his oil and replaced it with water. We rolled down the 101 Freeway and landed near a makeshift tent city near the Vine Street exit."

Chase appeared completely baffled. "Why didn't you tell me earlier? Are you hurt?"

"I've been better," I said.

Chase heaved an I'm-too-tired-and-stressed-to-ask-why-you-were-riding-in-a-car-with-your-baby-daddy-last-night sigh.

I kissed him before he mustered the energy to inquire. He reached for my neck and pulled me up by my waist until I was on my tiptoes. His lips parted, and our tongues met. He tasted like Chase. Sweet, sexy, strong, loving, Chase. And I felt breathless, in a good way this time.

We parted, and he went back to fighting crime. I wiped my nose and my eyes and rubbed my chest, all the while wondering if I had the stamina required for a love triangle.

# CHAPTER TWENTY-FIVE

———

*See also: Target*

"What an odd day," Tom said as he lowered himself to the couch.

"Odd? Try terrible." I was on the floor with gloves on, scrubbing pee stains out of the carpet. Like I'd been doing since Lilly went to bed. "Do they make diapers for dogs? I've seen Harold with a diaper on. If they make them for birds, they have to have them for other animals. Right?"

"Why don't you take him outside every twenty minutes to see if he has to pee so he knows that's where to go?"

"Because I'd look like a complete hypocrite. No dogs allowed. I can't give anyone here any more ammunition to move." Heaven knew they had enough. "He needs to pee over there." I pointed to the rental magazines sprawled out across the kitchen floor. Munch preferred carpet.

I coughed into my shoulder and sprayed Munch's latest deposit with cleaner and let it soak. "Looks like your Rent or Run page is down," Tom said, staring at his phone.

"Finally!" I peeled the gloves off my hands and checked

I'd received an email earlier from the admins at Rent or Run dot com and another from Yelp informing me our account had been frozen due to suspicious activity. Suspicious being the 5,000 one-star reviews left by loyal Jessica Wilders' fans.

*Five thousand!*

Which was roughly the same number of messages my mother had left on the office line.

Munch's little ears perked, and he barked at the wall. "Calm down, buddy." Tom rubbed his back. "There's nothing there." Munch settled beside Tom and resumed chewing on the

Barbie he'd been working on for the last hour, which was better than my kitchen table. He'd already gnawed on one leg.

I rose to my knees. "You two seem to have bonded."

Tom patted Munch's head. "He's a good dog."

"You should keep him," I said.

"I don't know if I could handle a dog."

"Too much of a commitment for you."

"Ouch." Tom rubbed his heart.

"Speaking of commitment issues, I have a question for you. What was the original plan for last night? Lilly said you had an evil sparkle with lots of people to play with. I get the play, but what was the sparkle?"

"I had a present for you."

"And?"

"And…look, you're famous." Tom pointed the remote control to the television.

*Guess we're moving on?*

I turned to watch the television. Michelle M. Mitchell, Southern California's iconic channel 7 newscaster, sat behind her desk with a blue blazer on, her dark hair teased into a helmet and a picture of Jessica and Lance on the screen behind her. "Breaking news in the *Ghost Confidential* Murders. Shanna Roberts, a resident at this Los Angeles apartment complex…"

They cut to video of my apartment building with the yellow tape flapping in the strong wind. Had I known it was going to appear on national news, I would have had the fascia painted.

"…was taken in for questioning earlier today. According to our sources, Roberts is the half sister of Jessica Wilders." They cut to a picture of Amy's headshot.

*Oh hell.*

"Amy Montgomery, known for her roll as sultry medium Page Harrison on the hit show *Ghost Confidential*, is also a tenant at the same building. Police recovered numerous items belonging to Wilders from Montgomery's apartment." They cut to video of Amy crying from an episode two weeks ago when Page Harrison found her boyfriend cheating on her with a zombie. "A spokesperson for Amy Montgomery released the following statement. 'Ms. Montgomery had absolutely no involvement in the murders and is cooperating with the investigation. The police have yet to comment, but according to online blogger Dirty Dan, Montgomery's home was searched earlier, and the police recovered incriminating evidence from her vehicle.'"

Dirty Dan was annoying.

They cut to a picture of Jessica Wilders walking the red carpet at last year's Emmy Awards. She had on a silver dress with a plunging neckline, and a plunging backline, and a slit up to her hip. Like Edward Scissorhands designed it. They cut to a picture of Lance Holstrom at the Emmy's. He had on a purple velvet suit with a satin lapel. Like Barney designed it. "Sources close to Wilders and Holstrom say that Roberts had been jealous of her half-sister's success and had recently confronted Wilders at a fundraiser, where she was escorted away by security."

They cut to a video taken from a cell phone. Jessica and Lance were standing on a platform with their arms around an old lady who had a little dog on a leash. The old woman stepped down, and Shanna walked up holding Munch and the cat. Jessica's face fell, and she said something through gritted teeth before she called for security. The person taking the video made the comment, "What a diva."

Back to Michelle M. Mitchell. "Wilders' and Holstrom's camps have released a joint statement. 'We're indebted to the LAPD for their quick response and incredible attention to detail. All we want is justice for Jessica, Lance, and Zahra.' We're going live now to Skip Waters, who is at the scene. Skip?"

They cut to Skip, who was standing on our front lawn with the address visible behind him. Great.

"Thank you, Michelle. I'm standing here at the apartment complex where Shanna Roberts, Jessica Wilders' sister, lived. I have with me a neighbor and friend of Ms. Roberts." The camera zoomed out, and there beside him was Silvia Kravitz and Harold. I watched with one eye open, scared of what she was about to say.

"Were you surprised to hear about Shanna Roberts?" Skip held the microphone below Silvia's mouth, and Harold pecked at it.

Silvia tugged her robe closed. "Yes, I am. Quite frankly we should take into consideration that she has not been officially charged with anything yet. As far as I knew, she was an up-and-coming actress."

"Did she ever mention Jessica Wilders?" Skip asked.

"Not that I can recall. She did say she didn't like the show *Ghost Confidential*, but I don't either. It's terribly loud and disturbs my parrot."

Harold turned his backside to the camera and pooped down the front of Silvia's nightie.

"You have a little something…" Skip pointed to the green goop down Silvia's chest. Harold didn't like Skip's close proximity and flew into Skip's face. Skip yelped, his hair fell off his bald head, and he stumbled out of the shot. Silvia cocked her head and smiled into the camera. Her robe slipped off her shoulder, and a blurry dot covered her chest.

They cut back to Michelle at the news table. She sat gawking into the camera until an off-screen voice said *pssssttt* to get her attention. She rolled her shoulders and cleared her throat. "We will return after these messages."

I yanked the remote away from Tom and hit Mute. "That's it. I'm never renting another apartment again…why are you laughing?"

"Because that was hilarious." He doubled over. "Did you see Skip's face when the bird attacked?"

OK, that was kind of funny.

"And the bird crapped down her front, and she didn't even notice."

OK, that was also kind of funny. "He eats crackers out of her cleavage too. They're very close," I added.

Tom gave me a look of disbelief. "This place needs its own reality show."

"I think I'd rather stay away from cameras for now." I tossed the remote back to Tom. It sailed over his head and crashed against the wall.

What part of the brain was in charge of coordination? 'Cause mine was busted.

*First my phone and now the remote.*

"That's it! Today is officially over. I'm done. I need to take a shower and go to bed. When are you going home, by the way?"

Tom put Munch on his lap and scratched behind his ears. "I'm staying here tonight."

"I don't think that's such a good idea."

"Why not?"

"Because I'm involved."

"Didn't seem like it this morning."

"You caught me at a weak moment." I rose to my feet and threw the gloves on the ground. "You should go home."

Munch put a paw on Tom's leg and whimpered.

"Traitor," I said to him.

Tom gave me a guess-I'm-staying shrug of his shoulders.

"Whatever. I give up. You both are sleeping on the couch. I'm going to take a shower. You stay put."

Tom gave me a captain salute.

I walked down the hall and into my room and locked the door behind me. I didn't trust Tom.

OK, fine. That was a lie. I didn't trust myself.

I turned on the shower and deposited my clothes into a pile on the floor. I let the hot water fall on my face and warm my skin. My thoughts turned to Shanna Roberts. When I'd run her credit check, an apartment in Downtown did show on her report. When I did a rental verification, her manager appeared genuinely surprised that Shanna was moving. Not a red flag. Most people didn't give notice on their current apartment until they'd found another. It seemed, to me at least, that Shanna used Apartment 17 for the sole purpose of being close to Amy. Which explained why she didn't have furniture. She never intended to live there.

I brushed the water from my eyes, grabbed the bottle of Pantene, and squirted a dollop into my palm. I lathered the soap in my hands when...crap. Shampoo!

I'd completely forgotten about what Shanna had written in her notebook. I stared down at my hands and screamed. Panicky, I rinsed the soap and turned off the shower. I grabbed towel, wrapped it around my chest, and fell into Tom.

"What's wrong?" He had me by the shoulders.

"I thought I locked the…" My eyes went to the bedroom door that was now split down the middle. "Did you kick in the door?"

"I heard you scream. What's wrong?"

"My shampoo," I said.

Tom clutched his chest. "You screamed because you're out of shampoo?" He sounded angry and relieved in the same breath.

"No, my shampoo. In Shanna's notebook she wrote that she did something to my shampoo. I forgot to tell Hampton when they interviewed me. As a matter of fact, I forgot all about it until just now when I was about to use my shampoo."

"Why would she do something to your shampoo?"

"I don't know. Why would she kill her sister? We're obviously not dealing with a sane person here." I tightened the towel wrapped around my chest, tucked the corner into the top, and walked to the kitchen. Tom followed.

"What are you doing now?" he asked.

I pulled the box of gallon Ziplocs from the cabinet. "I need to seal the shampoo and give it to Chase."

Tom and Munch followed me back to my bathroom. "Why are you taking out the whole drawer?"

I emptied the contents into a bag. "If she touched my shampoo, who knows what else she tampered with. Not worth the risk." I tossed my deodorant in next and sealed the bag.

Tom grabbed my arm so hard my hand tingled. "Shampoo?"

"Yeah, my shampoo. Why?"

Now he had me by the shoulders. "In the notebook, what did it specifically say?"

"It said *Cambria shampoo* with a checkmark. Why?"

"*Shampoo* or *shampooed*?" Tom asked.

I was about to say, "Does it matter?" But by the look on Tom's face, it mattered. "I'm pretty sure it said *shampoo*."

"Get dressed." Tom paced out of my room and into Lilly's.

"What are you doing?" I chased after him, holding tight to the corner of my towel.

"We're going down to the police station now." He flipped on Lilly's light. She didn't even flinch.

This was very un-Tom-like behavior. He could be counted on to be the rational, let's-think-things-through person in any given situation.

"You're scaring me," I said.

He collected clothes for Lilly, shoved them into her backpack, and zipped it up. "Go get dressed, Cambria."

Tom only used my full name when he was mad or it was urgent. I assumed it was the latter and didn't ask questions. I went to my room and shimmied into a pair of pants. My dampened skin made it difficult to pull the denim over my hips, but I managed. I put the grungy sports bra and purple shirt back on and ran back to Lilly's room.

"Tell me what's happening?" I asked Tom.

"Shampoo is another word for hit."

"Hit what?"

"It means Shanna hired someone to kill you."

"What?" I almost laughed. "No way. Why would shampoo be code for a hit man?"

Tom grabbed Lilly's Mickey Mouse doll. "Washed out of your life," he said. "I've spent the last six weeks researching this subject. I know what I'm talking about. Which means we all need to get to the police station now and demand protection."

I was down the hallway with Lilly flung over my shoulder before he finished his last sentence.

Lilly slept the entire journey to the living room. "Take her," I said to Tom, who followed behind with her stuff. "I have to set the alarm."

I passed Lilly off, typed in the alarm code, and set it for Away mode.

*Error message 345: Lobby door open.*

Crap.

"Hurry up, Cambria!" Tom said.

"I have to set the alarm this time." The wind must have pushed the lobby door, as the sensors weren't aligned, not allowing the alarm to set. I ran into the office and—*bam!*

The end.

# CHAPTER TWENTY-SIX

---

*See also: Swiss Cheese?*

Of my kneecap.

I collapsed to the floor. I'd been in and out of that office hundreds of times (maybe thousands) and never rammed my knee into the desk before—a huge accomplishment given that my coordination was broken. I rolled around on the floor and pushed profanity through clenched teeth. It felt like a knife was stuck in my knee, and for a single moment that was all I could think about.

"Hurry up, Cambria!" Tom yelled.

Right. Going to die.

I crawled out to the lobby on my hands and good knee and gave the front door a hard push. It was already closed.

"Forget about the alarm!" Tom yelled.

I couldn't forget about the alarm. If someone was really out to wash me, then I had to be sure they couldn't get in when we were gone. I crawled to the back door and gave it a hard push. The door chimed.

*Bingo!*

The sensors were aligned. The alarm could be set.

Mission accomplished.

Munch let out a series of ear-piercing barks, and the lobby window shattered. Broken glass rained down on me, cutting my hands and face with tiny shards. I crouched into a ball. My mouth tasted of metal, and I realized I was bleeding. From where, I had no idea.

"Cambria, what's going on?" Tom said.

"Get out!" I screamed.

The second window shattered, and the door blew apart.

*Holy hell. Someone is shooting like a maniac!*

My fight-or-flight was strong. My brain told me to stand and run. Instinct told me to lay low. I went with the latter and army crawled through the office. I could smell the sharp sulfur from the gun.

Tom was crouched behind the kitchen counter, his long body wrapped around Lilly, with his phone at his ear. "We need assistance right away!" He reached out a hand and pulled me inside. I kicked the door closed.

Lilly regarded me with one eye open and lazily licked her lips.

"What's happening?" she asked.

"We're…looking for the spider."

"Oh." She lowered her head to Tom's shoulder.

That worked. I said a quick prayer of thanks for childhood amnesia.

Munch was up on the back of the couch, barking at an unseen target. I returned to my stomach and tried to crawl to him, but Tom grabbed my ankle to keep me from moving.

"Someone is shooting at us. I have my daughter here. Please send help now," Tom said to dispatch.

"Munch," I called. He didn't respond. Then I remembered that wasn't his name. "Come here, Rover!"

Munch was still up on the back of the couch, barking ou the window.

I kicked my leg free from Tom's grasp and army crawle across the floor, up to the couch, grabbed hold of Munch's almost nonexistent tail, and pulled him down. He wrestled to break free, barking uncontrollably. "Shhhhhh." I fought to keep him in my arms. "Stop moving." He managed to get away, climbed back up the couch, and growled.

A loud bang was followed by a faint burning smell, and suddenly smoke crept under the door.

"There is a fire now," I heard Tom say into the phone.

"Rover. Munch. Dog!" I called one more time. Munch ignored me, too busy barking at whoever was trying to shampo us. I grabbed his hind leg and dragged him down. He fought against me, kicking and scratching and clawing at the couch. W wrestled until I was able to get him in an arm wringer—or, *um,* paw wringer. With his little front leg over his head and my arm wrapped around his chest, I rolled to my back and scooted to the kitchen. Munch yelped, but it was better than him getting shot in the head.

Tom pulled us in to the cocoon he'd made around our daughter. "We need to get out of here," he said.

"But if we go out the front, we could get shot."

"I hate shots," Lilly said.

I put my forehead to her. "Not that kind of shot, baby. We were just…just kidding. Bad joke."

"Like the chicken crossed the playground joke?"

"Exactly." I couldn't help but smile. "I'm a bad joke teller."

She wiped sleep from her eyes. "Yeah, you are."

More smoke slithered under the door into the kitchen, and it was clear this was no wax-melt fire. The building could very well burn down.

"Let's go back to your patio," Tom said. "We could take shelter in there."

He coughed. I coughed. Lilly coughed. Munch barked.

I pulled Lilly's shirt up over her nose. "We're going to pretend to be ninjas. OK?"

Lilly gave me a skeptical look but went along with it anyhow. Tom went first with Lilly and crawled out of the kitchen, down the hall. I assumed the same scoot-on-your-back-with-a-wiggly-dog-strapped-to-your-chest maneuver. Effective, but slow. Once I made it to my bedroom, I assumed it was safe to get to my feet and run to the patio, where Tom was waiting with open arms.

I heard the sirens.

I smelled the smoke.

I tasted the blood in my mouth.

It sounded as if a band of bass drums were practicing next door, but it was just my heart pounding in my ears. My eyes darted around the patio in search of a weapon should our killer find us. A few rocks, leaves, a palm branch, ants, and the book I threw out there yesterday with the spider—*Princess and the Frog.*

Great. I could paper cut our hit man to death.

Tom pressed his face up against the wooden panels to peek through the cracks. "SWAT is here. A whole army of them have guns drawn and are marching through the gate…is that?" Tom gasped.

"Is that what?" I asked.

Tom shook his head and pulled the three of us in tighter. "Nothing." He exhaled and dug his chin into the top of my head. I closed my eyes and waited.

The patio door slid open, and detective Hampton peeked his head out. "You're fine now." He used a soothing yet authoritative tone. "We've got the guy. Now we need to get you all out of here. Come on."

Hampton helped me to my feet. I put pressure on my knee and collapsed. Hampton shoved his arm around my waist to help steady me. Tom took over as my crutch, and we limped down the hallway. Munch walked on his own accord, wagging his tale and trotting along proudly like the amazing guard dog he was. The living room was filled with a thin layer of smoke, and we all hunched over and coughed.

"Fire department is two minutes out," Hampton said.

*Two minutes?* A lot could happen in two minutes.

"We need to evacuate the nearby apartments," I told him.

"We've got it covered," he said.

Residents were congregated in the courtyard. It was late—past 11:00 PM—and everyone was in their pajamas. Tom and I collapsed onto the grass. Lilly and Munch took a seat on our laps.

"Wow!" Lilly said in awe. "That was crazy."

That was another word for it.

The flames poured out of the windows in a fury. We were a good fifty feet away, and I could feel the heat on my skin. Smoke filled my apartment, and I thought about running in to gather priceless belongings. Like Lilly's locks I'd saved from her first haircut, the apron Grandma Ruthie had made me the Christmas before she died, pictures, and old yearbooks. The stuff that could never be replaced. But then, I realized everything I needed was beside me. My family was safe. Everything else was just stuff.

Also, I couldn't move my leg.

# CHAPTER TWENTY-SEVEN

———

*See also: Just a girl standing in front of a building, asking it to stop catching on fire*

Thirty minutes later, flashes of blue and red lights alternated across the faces of the emergency service personnel going to and from the wreckage. The helicopter returned and hovered above the building, shining a bright light down on the parking area, where I assumed the person responsible for the shooting was still being apprehended. According to the fire captain, a bullet hit the hydroxyl machine and it exploded. Two fires in less than seventy-two hours. That had to be some kind of world record.

It felt like déjà-freaking-poo.

Same crap situation, different day.

Well, not quite the same. The first time was a wax melter, the second a maniac with a semiautomatic weapon. Minor difference.

The press caught wind, and the police worked quickly to set up steel barricades across the street to keep the sea of photographers and journalists at bay. A chorus of *click, click, click* came from the hundred or so cameras aimed at the building, and tiny microphones stuck out of the crowd like baby giraffes. Residents grouped behind the steel barricades and gave interviews to various press outlets. A small group of cameras were horseshoed around Silvia and Harold. The two relished in the spotlight.

I had Munch tucked under my arm and my eyes glued to the driveway. I suspected Chase was in the parking lot under the helicopter searchlight. I waited anxiously for him to emerge to be sure he was unharmed.

Tom and Lilly were checking out a "super-cool" fire truck. Lilly sat behind the steering wheel with a hat on and pretended to drive. She was in heaven.

Ironic, because it felt like we were in hell.

Luckily, the fire was contained to the lobby *and* office. My apartment sustained smoke damage. No one was hurt. Not physically anyway. I might never sleep again.

Munch barked and tried to break free. I held him tight. Hampton walked down the driveway and cleared a path for Chase to follow with…*Jack the Cadaver's guy?*

I shook my head and blinked.

Yep, still Cadaver's Jack.

Jack had on his wing-tipped shoes and suspenders. He limped along with his hands cuffed behind his back, his shirt ripped open, his right eye swollen, and blood dripping from his mouth. Chase had a firm grip on Jack's arm and steered him to the black sedan parked at the curb. The *click, click, click* symphony grew louder.

And suddenly it all made sense. Jack the Cadaver's guy, the man proficient in death, was the killer. Shanna must have known Jack, which was why they'd sent Amy to the Cadaver's parking lot. Jack had known she wouldn't be on any surveillance cameras. Shanna had asked why I hated her. First I'd taken the urn. Then I'd gone to Cadaver's looking for information to exonerate Amy. No wonder she'd wanted to wash me out of her life. The same way she'd washed Lance and Zahra.

If I hadn't gone to Cadaver's Caverns, I wouldn't have been on her radar.

In my periphery I saw Mickey behind the barricade. He stared at me with the same intensity as earlier. I was about to roll my eyes, when it suddenly dawned on me that Mickey's last name is Smith.

Mickey Smith.

Mickey had lived there so long, his file was three pieces of paper, and the copy of his driver license was unreadable. In the system he was Mickey Smith. On his lease he was Mickey Smith. His folder said Mickey Smith. But deep down in my subconscious, Michael Smith sounded right.

I knew the name sounded familiar!

I limped over to him with Munch still in my arms. "You doing OK, Mickey?" I asked.

The whites of his eyes had a yellowish hue to them, and his bottom lip quivered.

"The government is corrupt," he said.

"Probably." I paused to sneeze. "Mickey, did you know Shanna?"

He shook his head.

"Do you know Chase?"

He shook his head.

"Do you know something about what happened to Jessica Wilders?"

He pointed to Jack. "See, see, I saw the, the girl in Apartment 15 put an envelope in the cabinet the other morning. Then, then the guy with the suspenders came and took the envelope and put the urn there." Mickey shook his finger. "I thought it was bad because it wasn't Apartment 15's carport, but then I thought, maybe, maybe, they did that so, if they, they were caught, then it, it wouldn't be traced back to Apartment 17."

"Good point."

"Yeah, yeah, then you took the urn and, after you did, that girl in Apartment 15 showed up and looked, looked for it. She was mad and called, called the guy with the suspenders and, and accused him of taking the money and not giving, giving her the urn. She looked, looked all around. So I called the tip hotline and told them that I saw a guy put an urn in a carport."

"So you think Shanna, in Apartment 15, paid Jack, the guy with the suspenders, to kill Jessica Wilders and give her the urn," I asked.

"I think the government has implanted microchips into our brains and soon we'll all be zombies."

"Or that."

For the record: I still think he's ex-CIA.

\* \* \*

The black sedan left, and the helicopter followed. The police taped off the front of the building, and the CSI trucks arrived. Exhausted, I leaned against the hood of a police car with

Munch still tucked under my arm. I didn't have to turn around to know Chase was behind me. I could feel him there.

"I think it's time to seriously reconsider my life choices,' I said. "Or take a vacation. Or both."

Probably both.

Chase reached to put his arm around my shoulders. Munch barked and bared his crooked teeth. Chase retracted his arm. I guess Munch was Team Tom.

"It's not for common knowledge yet," Chase said. "But Shanna Roberts came clean, and she's looking at three counts of first-degree murder."

"What about Jack?" I asked.

"Again, between you and me and…what did you name the dog?"

"Munch."

Chase nodded, remembering. "Between you, me, and Munch, this is a twisted feud that goes way back."

He had my attention.

Chase looked around to be sure no one was within earshot. When the coast was clear, he spoke. "It was all about the urn. According to Shanna, she proposed they split the ashes, each getting half, but Jessica wouldn't do it. In the meantime, Jack—who not only works at Cadaver's Caverns but used to work on *Ghost Confidential* doing props and makeup—he and Jessica'd had a short-lived fling last year that ended on a sour note, and Jack was fired. You following me?"

"Yes, it sounds an awful lot like the plot to one of my television shows."

"Like *Ghost Confidential*?" Chase asked.

"I was going to say Jerry Springer, but close enough. How'd Shanna meet Jack?" "Tinder."

My mouth dropped. "You can find hit men on Tinder?"

"No. They went on a date, and didn't *hit* it off." Chase smiled, proud of his pun. "She had explained her history with Jessica Wilders. Jack had explained his history with Jessica. They bonded over their mutual hatred. He offered to steal the urn for a price. Shanna claims she had no knowledge that Jack planned to kill Jessica too."

"You buying that?" I asked.

"Nope."

"Good. Me neither. Go on."

"She claims that once Jessica was killed, Jack had to kill Zahra because she knew too much about Shanna and Jessica's relationship."

"What about Lance?"

"This is where it gets Jerry Springer-esque. Jack killed Lance because *they* too had had a short-lived fling last year that didn't end well. Not sure if the flings were at the same time and that's why they ended. I'll let your imagination fill in the blanks."

Ugh. I had a pretty wild imagination.

"So now they'll both be charged?" I asked.

"Let's put it this way. You don't have to worry about them anymore."

"Good." The whole thing gave me a stomachache. "At what point did I become a problem in this?"

"When you took the urn and snooped around Cadaver's Caverns. CSI found the part about you being shampooed in the notebook and notified me immediately."

"*Pffft.* You were about fifteen minutes too late."

Chase frowned. "We need to work on our timing."

"No joke," I said. "Where is the urn, by the way?"

"It's at the station. We'll notify whoever is handling Jessica's property to come get it."

"And Mickey said he called the tip hotline and told you everything he saw in the carports. Why didn't you follow through?"

Chase gave me a look. "You can't possibly be talking about Michael Smith? That guy left a message saying he watched a man with suspenders take money. That's it. When we tried to interview him he wouldn't talk to us, said we were corrupt."

"Yeah, that sounds like Mickey." I moved Munch to my other arm. "I'm pretty sure he's ex-CIA."

Chase laughed. "I'm pretty sure he's a retired mailman."

"It's a cover."

"At this point, I'd believe just about anything."

Munch barked and squirmed to break free from my grasp. I looked up. Tom approached with Lilly on his back. She had on a red plastic firefighter hat, a golden police sticker stuck to her chest, and a huge smile on her face.

Tom unhooked Lilly's arms from around his neck and put her on the ground. "Thanks for looking out for us," he said to Chase. "I saw you run past the armed SWAT team to take out the shooter. That was ballsy."

Chase shrugged his shoulders like it was no big deal.

"What does ballsy mean?" Lilly asked.

"It means stupid," I said and shot Chase a look. "I'm all for a heroic effort on my behalf, but running past a heavily armed SWAT team to take out a heavily armed cadaver specialist *was* stupid. You could have gotten yourself killed."

"I'll never be ballsy, Mommy," Lilly said. "*Never*. 'Cause when I grow up, I don't want to be an idiot."

"That's a good goal," Chase said and gave her a high five.

"What's an STD?" she asked.

Both Tom and Chase looked at me.

"*Ummmmm*, it's not me...I'm good."

"You get them in jail," Lilly added.

"What are you letting her watch?" Tom asked.

Before I could answer, Munch leapt into Tom's arms and began to obsessively lick Tom's face.

"Looks like your dry spell is over," I said.

Tom rolled his eyes. "What's going to happen to this dog, anyway?" he asked Chase.

"There's protocol when it comes to pets. It's not my area of expertise, but I assume he'll go back to the shelter."

"What's a shelter?" Lilly asked.

"It's a place where animals that don't have homes go," I said.

Her little eyes watered, and she looked up at Tom. "Daddy, you can't let hers go to a shelter." She clasped her hands together. "Please, Daddy. Pleeeeeaaasseee."

"Thanks, Cam," he said under his breath.

"You're welcome."

Kevin appeared out of nowhere with his phone on a selfie stick. "I'm with Cambria Clyne, the apartment manager and Amy Montgomery's best friend." Kevin put his arm around my shoulders and brought me into the shot. "Cambria, do you have anything to say?"

"Get the camera away, or I'll punch you in the face."

"I'm live," he said through a smile.

"Fine. Amy Montgomery had nothing to do with this. And who are we live to?"

"My blog," Kevin said. "This is Dirty Dan reporting live. I'll be back with more." He stopped recording, and I punched him in the arm.

"Ouch. What did you do that for?"

"You're freaking Dirty Dan. What is wrong with you?"

"It's your fault."

"How so?"

"If you hadn't thrown away my plants, then I wouldn't have had to find a new source of income."

"What plants?" Chase asked.

"W-e-e-d," Lilly answered. "Mommy didn't waters them."

*Oh for heaven's sake, I'm officially done with today.*

# CHAPTER TWENTY-EIGHT

———

*See also: Zookeeper*

It had been three months since the last time the lobby burned down, and life had finally returned to normal.

*Normal* in a relative sense.

After the shooting, and fire, and media blitz (oh my!), I was left with six vacancies. That was a 15 percent vacancy rate. Neither Patrick nor Trevor held it against me because, as Trevor put it, "A lesser soul would have deserted this place months ago."

Pretty sure a smarter soul would have quit months ago, but I was still there, plugging along, collecting rent, filling out work orders, muddling through complaints, and renting apartments.

I was down to one vacancy.

Shanna's old unit.

"The kitchen is really big," Julia said to her brother, Kane. The brother and sister duo had come in an hour before to tour an apartment. They were looking to cut costs and bunk together in a one-bedroom. He would get the living room. She would get the bedroom. Not a terrible idea.

Julia had short, spikey red hair, and Kane had short, spiky blue hair. Both had rings in their noses and lips, and Julia confided in me that she'd recently pierced her nipples, even though I clearly didn't ask for that information. But who cared? Her entire body could be one big piercing so long as she wasn't murderer, psychopath, drug dealer, or parrot owner and she paid her rent on time.

"Julia, look at the bathroom," Kane said, and the two marveled at the long vanity and spacious setup.

"Our one-bedroom apartments utilize every inch of square footage to give you a spacious floor plan with maximum storage," I said in my best sales-pitchy voice. "You won't find another apartment like this under three grand in Los Angeles."

"It is a good price." Kane opened the hall closet. "What the…" He picked up a bobby pin painted white.

*Note to self: make sure the painters look* before *they slather on the paint.*

*Sub-note to self: ask them to stop watering down the paint too.*

*Sub-sub-note: find new painters.*

"I like it," said Julia. "This place has great reviews on Rent or Run dot com too."

"We aim to keep our residents happy," I said with a smile. It was hard to rebuild our reputation after it had been blasted on national news, but surprisingly easy to open new gmail accounts, create new profiles on Rent or Run dot com, and leave fake reviews.

Just call me CJ Vanilla or JC Roads.

"This apartment also has a big balcony. Right out here." I led them into the master bedroom and out to the balcony that, according to our brochure, was "an entertainer's dream!" If the entertainer only had three friends.

"It's big, but the view sucks," Kane said.

"I like it." Julia cupped her hands around her eyes like they were binoculars. "You can easily see into the apartments next door. Great people-watching opportunity. Look. That guy is about to take a shower."

The three of us squinted to get a better look and, yep, big, hairy man about to step into the shower. But first, he had to inspect his backside in the mirror.

"You could easily fit a table and propane grill out here," I said, in hopes of turning their attention away from the big, hairy man who was now doing squats.

"I like it. What's the deposit?" Julia asked.

"You're in luck. Right now we're running a move-in special. *Ifyouqualify* it will only be a five-hundred-dollar move-in, and that includes deposit and first month's rent."

"Five hundred?" they replied together.

"I mean, that's cool," said Kane. He tried to play it cool, but I knew I had them. "What about four hundred?"

"Four hundred, plus one hundred, will get you in. *Shouldyouqualif.* I can waive your application fee if you're approved today."

Kane and Julia looked at each other and said, "We'll take it."

\* \* \*

Kane and Julia admired the landscaping as we walked back to the office. It was a beautiful day. No clouds. No wind. "Blue sky and 87 degrees," per morning weather report. The buds had blossomed into poppies, geraniums, and iceberg roses. The ivy was lush and covered the breezeway in rich leaves and pink flowers.

We saw Kevin sorting through a stack of mail. He had his backpack slung over his shoulder and his work uniform on— *Gus's Cleaning Crew.* Tom had helped Gus with his legal woes. Gus had been the one who'd been accused of hiring a hit man to kill his boss. He'd been exonerated, thanks to Tom, and had opened his own cleaning company, since his boss was dead. He hired Kevin as a favor for Tom. It was "the crappiest job on the planet, maybe second only to yours," Kevin had said to me on his first day. But he was a rent-paying resident now. News he'd taken far better than I'd thought he would. It gave him the motivation to do something better with his life. He'd signed up for art classes at the local junior college. He planned to put his age-and-weight-estimating skills to use as a police sketch artist someday. Until then, he kept track of my ever-fluctuating weight. Today I was 129.

I never did tell Amy that Kevin was Dirty Dan because again, I didn't want to deal with any more murders.

"Hi, Kevin," I said as we passed.

Kevin grunted a greeting without looking up.

"Who's *that*?" Julia turned around and watched Kevin kick the pool gate closed with his shoe.

"That's Kevin. His parents own the building."

"And he lives here?" She bit at her lip.

*Good luck.*

Though, selfishly, if Kevin had another friend to hang out with, then who would watch *If Only* with me on Monday nights? We were about to find out who Bobbie Dart would choose—her newly resurfaced husband or the detective.

Kevin was rooting for the husband.

I was rooting for the detective.

Kane, Julia, and I stopped at the first laundry room to have a look around. The machines were all going, and Sophie from Apartment 38 was inside cleaning the windows. She'd fallen into a bit of trouble after a customer had received a bad essential-oil concoction. According to the legal papers, the plaintiff turned blue after spritzing himself with the Weight Loss Blend.

Sophie needed cash. I didn't need any more vacancies. Plus, I hated cleaning the laundry rooms. And now that Mr. Nguyen was both the maintenance man and training to become a maintenance supervisor over multiple properties, the laundry rooms were my responsibility. I assigned them to Sophie, gave her twenty bucks a month, and everyone was happy.

Except for Tam in Apartment 7. He was the one who turned blue.

"It's cool you have two laundry rooms," said Kane.

Julia ran her hand along the washing machine. "I hate lugging my stuff to the laundromat."

"It's a wonderful place to live," Alexis from Apartment 28 chimed in. She was sitting on the counter, waiting for her clothes to dry and stroking the doxie-poo on her lap.

I'd learned a doxie-poo was half-dachshund and half-poodle. After she'd filed for divorce from Trent, her therapist had said a dog would help her not want to kill her husband. She had a note from her doctor, and Patrick said there was nothing we could do, and I didn't want to deal with any more dead people. Once the doxie-poo entered the community, Apartment 8's podiatrist prescribed her a cat. Apartment 12's chiropractor said he had to have a yorkipoo. (Apparently, you can breed a poodle with anything and call it a "poo." And no matter how much poo was in a dog, I was still allergic).

In short, I hadn't taken a deep breath since March.

I didn't mind, too much.

After my interactions with Munch, I got it. Animals are great companions. I looked into getting a hairless dog myself but—*holy poo*. They cost around eight hundred dollars.

You'd think there'd be a discount since they didn't come with fur.

I got my animal fix whenever I went to Tom's. Munch was a great companion for him and, based on the bra I'd found in his couch the last time I visited, Tom's dry spell was over. I never did receive, nor find out, what the sparkle was.

\* \* \*

Back in the office, I pulled an application from the file cabinet and placed it on the newly installed counter. "I'll need three months of pay stubs from you both and copies of your driver's licenses," I said.

Kane and Julia clicked their pens and filled out the applications.

Once done, they each said "I'm done." And pushed the papers across the counter.

"By the way, I like the orange." Julie pointed her pen to the accent wall.

"Thank you. We're in the process of remodeling." As if the tarps, sawdust, exposed beams, and two electricians currently working didn't speak for itself. It had taken a while to get the insurance money. Filing two claims for the same room over the span of two days had raised a few red flags.

I did get a new desk. It was a bamboo, fully adjustable standing or sitting desk. Someday I planned to stand while I worked. My knee was still wonky. And by wonky, I meant it clicked when I walked and locked when the temperature dipped below seventy.

I should probably see a doctor about that.

Amy opened the door and peeked her head in. "Sorry to interrupt, but don't you have to leave soon?"

Yes, but I was renting an apartment here. *Priorities!* I wanted to say, but instead said, "I'll be right in."

"Was that Amy Montgomery from *Ghost Confidential*?" Julia asked. "Her death scene this week was—*wow*! I didn't see that one coming."

"Neither did we." A piano to the head, then her ghost was sentenced to eternal damnation. In short: there was little hope for a comeback. Even without Lola and Frank, the show continued. The ratings were higher than ever.

"If that was Amy Montgomery, then..." Kane took a step back. "Is this the apartment complex that was on the news?"

*Ugh.* "It is," I admitted. I'd lost way too many prospective residents once they'd figured it out.

Kane's face lit up. "That means Crazy Bird Lady lives here?"

Crazy Bird Lady, aka Silvia Kravitz, had become a meme and GIF star.

"I can't give out personal resident information," I said.

"So you're saying she does still live here?" Julia asked, hopeful.

"I can't confirm or deny."

For whatever reason, the possibility of being neighbors with Crazy Bird Lady sold them. (They obviously hadn't met her yet.) They turned in their paycheck stubs, signed the rental verification permission slip, and I made a copy of their driver licenses.

We said our goodbyes, and I locked the door behind them.

Amy was in my newly painted and carpeted living room, lounged across my new ultra comfy gray chaise couch. (It pays to have renter's insurance, just as it pays to have smoke damage.) Amy had on a wide-rimmed hat and flowy sundress, like she was sitting poolside at the Four Seasons, not here to babysit. She pointed the remote at the television and pressed the Off button with no luck. "This thing is busted." She pounded it against the palm of her hand before giving up.

"I think I rented my last apartment," I said.

"Shanna's?"

I nodded.

"Did you ever hire an exorcist?" she asked.

I'd looked into it, but exorcists were expensive. "No, but I put salt in the corners."

"That should...oh no!" Amy squealed in horror. "Can you believe this?" She pointed behind me.

"What now?" I turned around. On the television screen was a commercial for the *20/20* episode about the *Ghost Confidential* Murders. Amy's face took up the entire screen. It was footage of her leaving the police station after her last interview. Tom was at her side. She had on big-rimmed sunglasses and a floppy hat. She'd had an allergic reaction to the seaweed wrap, and her face was covered in welts. Not a good look.

"My name has been cleared. Why do you keep bringing me into this? Find a new story!" Amy screamed at the television.

I grabbed the remote and hit Pause. "Isn't any publicity good publicity?"

"Not when it involves murder!"

Good point.

I pushed Play. The deep voice-over announced, "We'll take a closer look at all parties involved. Into the life of Jessica Wilders before she achieved fame and fortune." They cut to the same picture I'd found in Shanna's box, the one of Jessica and Shanna with their charm bracelets on and Katherine behind them. "We'll look at Lance Holstrom." They cut to a picture of Lance on the beach with a coconut drink in his hand and a smile so big you could almost see every single one of his bleached teeth. "And the assistant who knew too much." They cut to a picture of Zahra. She was a short middle-aged woman with dark skin and dark hair streaked with gray. Not at all like the Zahra I pictured in my head. In my head Zahra looked like Ellen DeGeneres. Not sure why. Ellen's my go-to actor when visualizing people.

"It's been three months. You'd think news would die down by now." Amy bit at her nail beds. "It's probably because of the stupid movie."

"What stupid movie?"

Amy gawked at me. "You haven't heard about the movie?"

"No!"

I had my new phone out. According to Google, Lifetime had *The Ghost Confidential Murder* movie in production. I scrolled through the cast list on IMDb.

Jessica Wilders played by Anna Paquin.

*Meh.* I could see the resemblance if you squinted your eyes and tilted your head to the side.

*Scroll*

*Scroll*

*Scroll*

Amy Montgomery played by Julianne Hough.

Oh geez. Not that Julianne Hough was a bad choice. It was further proof of how badly Amy's career had tanked. She couldn't even land the role as herself.

*Scroll*

*Scroll*

*Scroll*

Detective Cruller played by Chace Crawford.

I could see the resemblance.

*Scroll*

*Scroll*

*Scroll*

Apartment manager, Cam, played by...

"David Spade!" Not that there was anything wrong with David Spade, other than the fact he was a man and I was a woman. "This is ridiculous! Stupid producers." I tossed my phone onto the couch. "I hate Hollywood."

"Hear, hear." Amy wiped away a tear. "Aren't you going to be late?"

I checked my watch. "Not if I leave now and don't hit any traffic."

"Are you wearing that?"

I looked down at my jeans, Converses, and blue shirt. "No?"

# CHAPTER TWENTY-NINE

———

*See also: David Spade*

I took the 5 Freeway and made it to Burbank in less than twenty minutes. I parked at the curb and climbed out of my car. As I stepped onto the sidewalk, I flattened the front of my dress with my hands and picked off the crushed Cheerios stuck to the bottom. I had on a blue Anthropologie dress, the one I'd worn when I first interviewed with Patrick last year. Fitting, given the situation.

Trevor had fired the Burbank apartment manager during the inspection. It had been three months, and they had yet to find a replacement. It was easy to see why. The position wasn't on-site, the pay was crummy, no benefits, no pool, no laundry room, no parking, 32 units, and three vacancies, with two notices on file. Seasoned managers wanted nothing to do with it, and those who had applied weren't qualified. I wasn't sure at what point Patrick thought, *This place is a hot mess, the situation is dire, no one will take the job...you know who would be perfect? Cambri Clyne.* But he had called the week before to offer me the position over the phone. The deal was I'd manage both communities for slightly more pay, plus gas money. It wasn't the golf cart I was hoping for, but it was a step in the right direction.

Before I could accept the offer, I had to look at the property to be sure it was a good fit for me. The fact I had to park three blocks away wasn't a good start, but the fact that I barely made it one block before I had to stop and catch my breath told me the forced exercise wouldn't be a bad thing.

The street was lined with apartment buildings on both sides, cars were parked along the curbs, and the sidewalks were busy with women jogging, men pushing strollers, college-aged kids with a script in one hand and pulling a cart of groceries with the other.

I arrived at Building 414 feeling a bit winded. I could tell the property had been without a manager. The *Now Leasing* sign was dirty, there were cobwebs in the windows, and the gutters needed to be cleaned. Details only a trained eye would notice. Other than that, it was a nice place.

The building was a two-story Spanish style with clean landscaping and a towering palm tree in the front. There was no security gate, and I walked under an archway, past the mailboxes into the courtyard. I did a slow spin to take in the surroundings. I counted forty-two infractions. Charcoal BBQ pits, wet laundry flung over the railing, chalk drawings on the walkways, ashtrays by the front door.

"These people are going to hate me," I said under my breath as I did another spin around.

At least I wouldn't live here, so they could hate me all they wanted Tuesdays and Thursdays from nine to five. Then I could go home. Not a bad gig for an extra ten grand a year. My only reservation was the close proximity to Warner Bros. Studios. I had a hunch most who lived here were starving actors. And I'd sworn off Hollywood.

I checked my watch. I was going to be late, but I had a good feeling about this. I could turn this place around. Before I'd left, I'd called Patrick to let him know. "I'll take it."

\* \* \*

I parked at the police station, climbed out of my car, and called Chase to tell him I was there. He told me he'd be right out and to meet him by his car, which was all fine and dandy, except there were ten black sedans parked in the back and I had no idea which one was his. I assumed we were taking a work vehicle since this was official police duty.

I assumed wrong. My phone rang from the depths of my purse, and the screen told me it was Chase.

"Where are you?" he asked.

"Waiting by the assembly of black sedans."

"We're taking my car."

I looked around and saw Chase across the parking lot waving his arm to get my attention. He was dressed casually: jeans, white hoodie, black baseball cap on his head. With the urn in his hands.

"Why aren't you more dressed up?" I asked.

"Because we're not going to a funeral."

Fair enough.

Chase drove a black Jeep Wrangler Rubicon. He opened the passenger door for me, and I slid in and buckled my seat belt. Chase climbed into the driver's side and passed over *Mom*. I put her on my lap and held on with two hands.

"You sure about this?" Chase asked.

"I'm positive. Now drive."

He typed the address into the GPS, and the automated woman's voice directed us to take the 405 north. Jessica's father didn't want the urn back. He'd told Chase to burn it. Poor Mr. Wilders had no idea how badly that would end for him. The next person *Mom* would go to was Shanna, who was in prison for the foreseeable future. The urn had sat in the police station until Chase was able to find the next of kin, which wasn't easy. Katherine Roberts was an only child, and her parents had died when she was a teenager. Finally, after three months of searching, and three months of me pestering him, Chase had found a cousin in Calabasas who said she'd happily take Katherine's remains. And he asked if I would like to deliver the urn personally.

I'd said, "No."

Then he asked me again, and I replied with, "Hell no."

By the third time, I gave in.

Katherine's cousin lived in a gated community not far of the freeway. We had to provide photo identification to the security guard working the booth, before the golden gates would part. The cousin's mansion was at the top of a hill overlooking the valley. Chase pulled into the circular driveway, and we took a moment to marvel at the grandeur. It looked as if it were cut from *Beverly Hills Living* magazine. Everything about the home was grand. The marble fountain out front, beaming white columns, bushes trimmed into perfect squares. The balconies were bigger than my apartment, and the front door was made of glass and stood at least fifteen feet tall.

If Katherine was still disturbed here, then there was no pleasing her.

I rang the doorbell, and a beautiful melody of chimes echoed from inside. Chase put a hand on my lower back while we waited. We saw the silhouette of a person walking down a winding staircase toward the door. She stopped to speak to another silhouette before she answered.

My heart leapt into my throat, and I made some sort of strangled sound as the door opened. It was Bobbie Dart from *If Only*. Bobbie Dart played by...by...by...Sandy Roberts. I'd never been more starstruck in all my life. Or dumbstruck. I forgot how to speak. So Chase took over for me.

"Hello, Mrs. Roberts. My name is Detective Chase Cruller, and this is Cambria Clyne."

Sandra had long black silky hair, big brown eyes, dark skin, and a smile that lit up a room. She took *Mom* from me and invited us to stay for tea in the library. Even though Chase and I had dinner plans, and even though I didn't drink tea, I eagerly replied, "Yes!" Because how often are you invited to tea with your favorite television star?

Sandra's library was a circular room with floor-to-ceiling books. Four cozy-looking leather armchairs were positioned around a small coffee table that looked as if it belonged in an ancient Greek castle. A short woman in jeans and a high ponytail, who I assumed to be the maid, brought in a tray heavy with teacups and a kettle.

The three of us took a seat. The leather felt like butter against my skin, and I wanted to curl up and take a nap. Sandra poured us each a cup of tea. The tea tasted like watered-down grass, but when Bobbie Dart offers you tea, you drink it. And you like it.

"Are either of you readers?" Sandra asked.

"I read casually," Chase said. "I know Cambria is. She keeps a copy of *Pride and Prejudice* in her nightstand."

Sandra's eyes gleamed at this news.

Oh hell.

"My all-time favorite book. Don't you just love Jane Austen?" she asked.

"Who doesn't?" I said. "Mr. Darcy is my favorite character."

"Agreed." Sandra crossed her ankles and sipped her tea. "It was so nice of you to go through so much trouble to be sure Katherine was returned to family."

"It was Cambria's doing," Chase said. "She was adamant that the urn be returned."

"I felt it only right that she rest in peace amongst family." Also, I couldn't risk being cursed any longer. But I didn't say that, and it's not as if I truly believed in all that...*that* much anyway.

"I was so sad to hear about Jessica," Sandra said. "I'd met her a few times at various events, but she didn't want anything to do with me. She looked so much like her mother. Katherine and I grew up together. She was not only my cousin but also my best friend. We lost touch after high school. She got into drugs, and I went off to college."

"Did you ever meet Shanna?" Chase asked.

Sandra dabbed her mouth with the edge of a white linen napkin. "No. I was unaware Katherine had a second daughter. I knew about Jessica. And I knew Jessica's father had custody of her and that Katherine had struggled with drugs. Had I known about Shanna, I would have been inclined to help her."

Ironic, I thought. Shanna had a famous half sister, who wanted nothing to do with her, and an even more famous second cousin who would have been willing to help.

"I'll keep Katherine safe until Shanna can get her." Sandra hugged the urn.

"That might be awhile," Chase said. "She's looking at twenty-five to life."

"You're right. I knew that. I read it in *Daily C-Leb Mag.* Did you hear about the movie?"

"It sounds terrible," I mumbled under my breath.

"Cambria is a big fan of your show, *If Only*," Chase said.

I shot him a look. Why would he tell my favorite actress that I liked her show...and, well, I guess that was a good thing.

"How wonderful," she said. "Are you excited for the finale on Monday?"

"I can't wait," I said, trying to play it cool. "I'm dying to find out who she ends up with—the cop or husband?"

Sandra bit at her bottom lip to hold back a smile. "I can't give too much away, but I will tell you this. It's unlikely she will commit to one or the other until at least season four or five. The producers enjoy playing out the love triangle for as long as possible."

Darn.

We spent the next thirty minutes chatting *If Only*. Sitting in Bobbie Dart's library, talking about Bobbie Dart, was the coolest thing I'd ever done. Perhaps a thank-you sent from Katherine, not that I believed in all that...*that* much.

Sandra walked us out, and I waited until we were in the car before I said, "I can't believe we were inside Bobbie Dart's house! Did you know?"

"Why do you think I insisted on you coming?"

"I have to text Amy and tell her." I pulled out my phone, and Chase pried it from my grasp. "Hey, what did you do that for?"

"No Amy. Tonight it's you and me. We're finally celebrating your birthday."

"Oh yeah. What did you have in mind?"

Chase put his hand on my thigh. "I know what you want."

Oh boy.

*  *  *

I pulled the blanket up to my chin, lay my head on Chase's chest, and curled my arm around his waist. He nestled his face close and kissed my forehead. "Did you like that?"

"It was the best one yet."

"Really? I like *Taken 2* better."

"The truth is, Liam Neeson can make no bad movies."

"You make a good point." Chase reached over the side of the couch and grabbed the next DVD from our pile. "*The Commuter*?"

"Pop it in."

Chase started the movie and returned to the couch with two bowls of rocky road ice cream. He settled in beside me, and we cheered our spoons as the opening credits played. "Have you seen this yet?" Chase asked.

"Not yet. Why? Have you?"

"No."

"Do you think we'll actually watch it?"

"I hope not." Chase grabbed my bowl of ice cream and set it on the side table. He held my face between his hands and looked at me—really looked at me with his beautiful green eyes. I wrapped my hand around his neck and brought his mouth to mine. Our tongues met, our hands explored, my rocky road turned to liquid on the table, but I didn't mind.

I didn't mind one bit.

# ABOUT THE AUTHOR

Erin Huss is a blogger and best selling author. She can change a diaper in fifteen seconds flat, is a master overanalyzer, has a gift for making any social situation awkward and yet, somehow, she still has friends. Erin shares hilarious property management horror stories at *The Apartment Manager's Blog* and her own daily horror stories at erinhuss.com. She currently resides in Southern California with her husband and five children, where she complains daily about the cost of living but will never do anything about it.

To learn more about Erin Huss, visit her online at:
https://erinhuss.com

Enjoyed this book? Check out these other humorous mystery reads available in print now from Gemma Halliday Publishing:

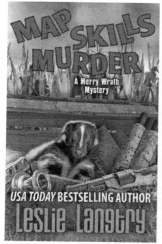

www.GemmaHallidayPublishing.com

48390570R00123

Made in the USA
Middletown, DE
13 June 2019